BLOCKER'S
BLUFF

GEORGE ENCIZO

ISBN –13: 978-1491042717
ISBN –10: 1491042710

CreateSpace Independent Publishing Platform
North Charleston, South Carolina
Printed in the United States of America

To my son, thanks for the inspiration.

Sometimes circumstances cause foolish people to do things that later cause dire consequence. Sometimes stupid people create conditions that eventually cause disastrous consequences to themselves and others.

The mundane may not always be exhilarating, but at least there is little peril. The alternative may be exciting, but it is often rife with dangers. It's always better to let your conscience be your guide.

BLOCKER'S
BLUFF

PROLOGUE

Charleston, South Carolina

Barbara Parker and her husband Tom arrived Wednesday afternoon at the Belmond Hotel in the historical district. Tom was mayor of Blocker's Bluff, owner of its bank and its only restaurant. He was there for the 2004 Southeastern Community Bankers' Conference—one of many he had attended during the past year. It wasn't something she had looked forward to but suspected that the conferences were more than what he said they were. She decided to find out for herself and went with him.

For the past year, Tom kept pushing her away. Their bedroom had become devoid of love, and she was certain he was having an affair either during the conferences or at home. There was more intimacy when her children were home, but now they were away at college. An empty nester at forty-six, she wasn't prepared for the loneliness he bestowed upon her. She was still attractive; her hair was still blond and hadn't gained more than ten pounds since high school.

Her parents paid for her to attend Clemson University to study art history. After her sophomore year, she decided to travel abroad with her parents and chose not to continue her education. Parker courted her for two years and at the age of twenty-five, she decided to marry him because of the social status he afforded her. She gave him two children and chose to be a stay at home mom to raise her son and daughter and never regretted it—until now.

After freshening up and changing clothes, they joined the other banker's and their wives in the ballroom for the welcoming reception. It didn't take long to realize it was a mistake coming to the conference. Tom immediately left her alone and joined some other bankers and their wives. Barbara attempted to mingle with a group of women.

She could tell immediately by the way they treated her that she was out of her element. Barbara was a bit of a snob herself, but the group of wives was downright boorish and preoccupied with themselves. When she mentioned she was from Blocker's Bluff, they asked where it was and told them it was in the low country. They frowned; obviously misunderstood her and assumed it meant where people were low class. Before she could explain that The Low Country was the geographic and cultural region that stretched south to Beaufort, they asked what she did there. When she said that she was a homemaker, they raised their eyebrows, turned, walked away, and ignored her the rest of the evening.

Not one to be daunted, she lifted her chin, saw a few men who were unaccompanied, walked over, and engaged them in light conversation. Occasionally she looked over at the other wives, tipped her glass and winked. They lifted their eyebrows and turned their backs. Barbara smiled feeling vindicated.

To make matters worse, Tom spent the evening glad-handing the other bankers and ignored her. When the reception ended, he caught up with her and asked if she was bored yet and if she realized it was a mistake to come. She feigned enthusiasm so as not to give him satisfaction. They walked to their room in silence. Later in bed, she attempted to engage in romance with him, but he said it was a long day tomorrow and needed to sleep. She rolled over on her side angry and frustrated.

The conference had arranged for a bus tour Thursday morning for the wives. She decided to go and bordered the bus. The women made sure there were no empty seats next to them, so she sat by herself.

Another wife sitting alone joined her and whispered, "Seems the others are ostracizing us." She drew out her vowels. "My name's Betsy Caldron, what's yours?"

"Barbara Parker." She tilted her head toward the other wives and grinned. "Looks like it. Ignore them. We'll be okay by ourselves. Where are you from, Betsy with that accent?"

Betsy's eyes lit up. "From a small town, you probably never heard of it." She leaned closer in and said. "It's not far from the Georgia Lowcountry. We're about two hours from Beaufort. My husband works at the local bank. We're going through a rough patch, and thought this weekend we would be good for us." She frowned and avoided Barbara's eyes. "So far it doesn't appear to be helping. What about you? I heard you were from a small town too."

Barbara grinned. "I am, I guess you heard me last night. I'm in a somewhat similar situation as you. How about we stick together today and have lunch by ourselves?"

"Sounds good to me." She drew her vowels out again.

The two women spent the tour together and instead of joining the other wives; they had lunch by themselves at a different restaurant. After lunch, they spent time in the lounge drinking Naughty Belles and whispering to each other lewd suggestions about their bartender.

Betsy checked her watch. "Oh my, it's almost time for dinner with the boys." Her speech was slightly off kilter. "Maybe we should go get ready. What do you think, Barbs?"

Barbara waved her hand and snickered. "The hell with them, Bets, let's go to dinner by ourselves."

"Okay, but what do we do?"

"We tell our husbands we spent too much time walking and don't feel up to going to dinner and say we prefer to stay in the room and order room service. They can go by themselves."

Betsy grinned. "Oh, I like that."

"I'll meet you in the lobby at 6:00. I'm going to take a quick nap, a shower, and then dress. Here's my room number. Call me when you're ready to go." She wrote it on her napkin.

"Whoo, I think I better do the same thing. I'll call you."

They walked to the elevator together and entered. Betsy leaned against the wall and removed her shoes. When the elevator came to her floor, she stepped out, held her shoes in one hand and waved the other as she teetered down the hallway.

"See ya, girlfriend."

Barbara went to her room, napped and then showered. When she stepped out of the shower, the phone rang.

"Hello."

A lingering silence and then, "Barbara, it's me, Betsy. I can't join you for dinner. My husband found me asleep and kinda intoxicated." She paused. "He got real angry, said I was an embarrassment, and we're going home." Her voice trembled as she continued whispering. "We're leaving after he finishes showering and gets dressed. I'm glad I met you and wondered if we could ever get together. You're not that far from me."

Barbara sensed there was something more but didn't ask. She was disappointed as now she had to go to dinner with Tom.

"I'm sorry, Betsy, it's all my fault. I shouldn't have kept you in the lounge so long."

"It's not your fault. I enjoyed myself and your company. I haven't had such fun in a long time."

"We didn't do much except drink and ogle that bartender."

"Yeah, he was hot!"

"He sure was. Betsy, here's my phone number. Call me some time; maybe we could get together." She gave Betsy her number. "Betsy wait, what do you do in that town where you live?"

"I'm and English teacher and in my spare time, I'm writing a mystery."

"That's great; I wish I had your talent. Goodbye, Betsy."

"Goodbye, Barbara."

Later Tom arrived and asked what she did during the day.

"I took a bus tour with the other wives and then I walked around the city." She put her hand on her forehead. "I think I may have gotten too much sun. If you don't mind, I'd like to order room service and stay in." She searched his face for disappointment, but it was blank. "You go to dinner without me."

"That's fine, you relax. I'll see you later." Tom showered, dressed and left. Barbara ordered room service and watched Wheel of Fortune and Jeopardy.

That night when they were in bed, Barbara reached over and tried for some affection, but once again he pushed her away. He said he had a long day tomorrow; it was a sports day. The choice for the attendees was golf or tennis. Since he didn't play tennis, golf was his choice. After the golf game, there was a dinner and cocktails at the golf course so he wouldn't be back until late in the evening.

Friday morning, Barbara purposely skipped breakfast to avoid the other wives and went to the fitness center for a morning workout. When she checked the hotel's website, it stated a small fitness center with a few treadmills and some free weights. She was unsure about using it, and hastily threw in shorts and one of the t-shirts for doing laundry when packing. Doing their laundry was okay but not housework as it was beneath her and would never think of stooping so low. Maybe she was just as pompous as the other wives.

Dressed in a loose pair of shorts and an oversized t-shirt, she was alone on one of the treadmills with headphones clinging to her ears and listening to soft music. She welcomed the solitude as she had nothing else to do with her time since Betsy had gone home.

Suddenly she wasn't alone. A man got on the treadmill next to her and greeted her.

"Good morning!"

She glanced at the workout display and noticed she still had twenty-five minutes to go. She politely responded "Good morning" in return and offered no further comment. She didn't recognize him from the previous night's reception, so chose to avoid any further comment.

"Are you here for the conference?" he asked.

She wasn't interested in making conversation and again glanced at the remaining time left for her workout. All she wanted was to be left alone with her thoughts; however, she didn't want to be impolite and responded.

"Unfortunately, I am, but only as the reluctant spouse. Are you here for the conference too?"

"Me? No! I'm a writer, and I'm doing some research. I meet some interesting people at hotels, and I hope to pick up some ideas for characters for my new book. Why do you say the reluctant spouse? Didn't you want to come here?"

She had only just met the man, yet for some strange reason, she felt compelled to unburden herself. It's not like they would ever cross paths again. He seemed like a charming man, similar in age, and she was curious about what it was like to be a writer.

"It was my idea. I suspect my husband has been fooling around, and I thought it was at one of the several conferences he attends." The words were out before she realized what she said. She considered changing the subject but decided to reveal her feelings. "This one is proving to be boring, and I've still got three days to go." She switched topics. "You must meet interesting people as a writer. What's it like being one?"

Sensing there was something deeper bothering this attractive woman, he decided to engage her in further conversation and offered her some insight.

"I do. Writing is fun and exciting, but it's also tedious work. If you don't have a passion for it, you quickly lose your trend of thought. When that happens, you get what's called writer's block."

She found herself pleased that he wanted to continue the conversation and wanted to know more.

He had plans for the day and decided to see if Barbara would like to be a part of them.

"So tell me, what are you going to do for three days? Spend all your time on the treadmill?"

"I don't know; I haven't given it much thought. Any suggestions?"

What harm could it be to ask? She just might find something to occupy her time. Whatever suggestions he had to offer, they would be better than spending another day in her room watching television and ordering room service.

Her time was up on her workout, but she quickly pressed start not wanting it to be obvious. The seconds started ticking away. He noticed her slyness, glanced her way and smiled. She smiled back with her infectious smile that could light up a room when she wanted to.

"Have you toured Charleston? There's much to see."

"'I took a bus tour yesterday with the other wives. I wasn't impressed." She suddenly found herself thrilled by their conversation and enjoying his company.

"Then you haven't explored Charleston and its history and charm in depth. There's so much to see and learn. What are your plans for lunch?"

"I haven't given it any thought yet. Why do you ask?"

He wondered if she would take the hint or shy away. Since he would be having lunch by himself, he decided to take a chance and invite her along.

"Well, if you don't mind me asking, I could use some company. You're welcome to join me as I explore Charleston and do some research. I promise you won't be bored."

She didn't have any plans and thought it just might be fun. It would certainly be better than how she spent the previous day.

"If you're sure you want company, and I won't be a nuisance, I'd love to join you."

"You won't be a nuisance: I can assure you." His smile sparked a sensation in her that she hadn't felt in quite some time. "My name is Alex. What's yours?"

"Barbara." She had that sensation again. "It's a pleasure to meet you Alex. Should we meet in the hotel restaurant?"

"Why don't we meet in the lobby, and I'll take you to a charming restaurant for lunch. Is twelve-thirty okay with you?"

"I'll meet you at twelve-thirty."

She had planned on only doing an hour on the treadmill, but having added more time and engaged in conversation, she completed almost two hours. The workout was exhilarating as was the conversation.

They finished their time on the treadmills then left for their hotel rooms. Barbara felt excited that, at least for one day, she had something to do.

At twelve-thirty they met and went to lunch in Alex's car. The restaurant he chose was quite charming and later he took her on a walking tour of Charleston. He gave her a pad and pencil and told her to take notes. Barbara was thrilled about it.

The historic district was ablaze with a profusion of color from the abundance of azalea bushes. They visited Charleston's old and historic district where there were some homes from the glory days of Charleston, and the not so glory days.

Almost every house had large flowerpots in the entry-way and window boxes filled with a variety of geraniums. It was as though the occupants were welcoming visitors to enter and enjoy the beauty and comfort of their homes. It made the two-hour tour so much more pleasant.

As they visited the various homes, Alex had a story about each occupant and their family secrets. Periodically he would tell Barbara to make a note of it. Alex accentu-ated the stories with humor, and she felt he might have embellished some. She was so engrossed in his tales and making little notes that she didn't mind.

She was just happy to be spending the afternoon with someone who appreciated her company, and she was fasci-nated by the whole experience. There was even a spark of infatuation.

When they returned to the hotel, Alex asked her if she would like to spend time again tomorrow morning explor-ing more of Charleston. She had no plans, so she said "yes" and they agreed to meet in the lobby at nine-thirty.

As they were about to board the elevator, Alex asked her what she was going to do the rest of the day.

"I don't have any plans because my husband's playing golf and having dinner at the golf club." She looked away to avoid him seeing her disappointment. "I'll be all alone the rest of the afternoon and evening."

Sensing she was lonely for affection, he invited her to help organize the notes and research material they had gathered. But that meant spending the afternoon in his hotel room.

"That's fine with me, that way I won't be alone and I'll have something to do." She was pleased that he had asked because she wanted to enjoy more of his company. He had a strange effect on her.

Alex ordered a bottle of wine from room service, and they spent the afternoon brainstorming ideas. She was fascinated by the whole process and didn't want to leave and have dinner by herself. She took a chance and asked.

"Alex, what are you doing for dinner this evening?"

"I don't have any plans. Would you like me to have dinner with you? We can order room service and another bottle of wine if that suits you, or we can go out?"

"Let's order room service." She was thrilled by the thought of spending more time in his room.

He warmed to her smile and ordered dinner plus another bottle of wine. When dinner arrived, he suggested they sit out on the balcony and enjoy the view.

"We have plenty of time; why not make the most of it?"

She suddenly found herself admiring him and wondered what it would be like to spend the night. It was a strange feeling for her. She knew at least she wouldn't be alone, and maybe he wouldn't push her away like her husband.

He sensed her thoughts and reached for her hand and just held it. For her, the feel of his hand in hers was electrifying. She felt a warm sensation and secretly hoped there was more to it.

Suddenly he leaned over and kissed her on the lips. There was another warm sensation as she let his lips linger on hers.

Alex pulled back. "I apologize; I didn't mean to do that."

"It's okay." Then she leaned over and kissed him. The sensation was both overwhelming and consuming. The kiss lingered for a while and then their mouths locked in a passionate embrace.

He led her to the bed, both undressed, and got in next to each other. When their bodies meshed, their mouths locked once again. She gave her complete self to him as he pleased her with something she'd never experienced before.

The whole experience was so new to her. She wanted to stay in Alex's arms forever, but, unfortunately, she had to get back to her room before her husband returned. "Alex, I haven't felt this alive in a very long time. I'm grateful for what you've given me."

"The feeling is mutual." He touched her cheek and rubbed his hand down her neck tenderly. "Since tomorrow is your last day, would you like to do something together?"

Her heart fluttered, she put her hand on his and took a deep breath to settle herself.

"Yes, but I don't have the evening available because there are a final dinner and celebration I must attend."

"That's fine. We'll just meet in the lobby again at nine-thirty if that's okay with you."

She was disappointed but agreed. That night all she could think about was Alex and seeing him once again.

The next morning they spent more time exploring. Afterward, both went back to Alex's room and replayed last night's scenario except there was more fire this time. Barbara was hungry for his offering and as she reached orgasm, she shouted, "I love you, Alex."

So overcome with pleasure, she decided to return the pleasure and did something she'd never done before—not even with her husband. It was her way of showing Alex that in the few days they'd known each other; she had indeed fallen in love. She was once again feeling alive, thanks to Alex.

When it was time to say goodbye, she told him about her feelings.

"I'm in love with you, Alex and would like to see you again."

He took her hand in his, kissed her tenderly on the lips and replied, "I feel the same way. May I have your telephone number? Maybe we can arrange something."

Since he was often in Charleston, they decided maybe next time they could get together.

She kissed him and said, "I'd like that. I'm going to miss you and would love to get together again."

Barbara left and went to her hotel room to prepare for the night's event. Alex closed the door and said, "This would make a great plot."

In the evening, she attended the dinner with Tom. He left her alone and wandered off to socialize with the other men and their wives. She galloped over to the men she met the first night and struck up a conversation with them. Unlike that first night, she had interesting things to say about her tours during the day and a writer she met. As she went on about her exploits, she kept thinking about Alex and when they might see each other again.

Sunday morning after breakfast, Barbara and Tom left the hotel and drove home in silence. He concentrated on the road; she gazed out the window worried about Betsy and wondering if she would ever see Alex again.

CHAPTER 1

Blocker's Bluff, a small coastal town of nine hundred residents, was located in one of the several inlets sandwiched between Beaufort and Charleston. It was on the far eastern edge of Crofton County just barely inside county limits. You won't find the town on any maps.

The town was named after Major Jeremiah T. Blocker who fell in an infamous battle during the Civil War. Blocker had been a member of the militia that garrisoned at the state arsenal in Charleston which later became The Citadel Academy. He had no battle experience but knew something about tactics. When word came that the Union army was approaching, he was selected to lead a band of local farmers and fishermen to defend their land and property. He appointed himself a major, mounted his horse and took charge.

What was supposed to be an army turned out to be a squad of soldiers led by a sergeant that had gotten lost and were sweltering from the heat in their wool uniforms. Prepared to mount a charge, someone fired their weapon inadvertently; the Major's horse took a bullet in the leg, went down and landed on the Major, killing him instantly. Without a leader, his ragtag troops decided it was no longer worth fighting. They were more interested in protecting their property than fighting. They decided what the hell, why continue?

They waved the white flag and offered to share a few jugs of moonshine with the Union troops. Their leader accepted the offer, removed their woolen tops, and joined their foe in gorging on a roasted hog and drinking hooch. Both sides had a good old time taking relief from the war. Afterward, they all went home.

After the war ended, a few sharecroppers and tenant farmers, who were fortunate to purchase their land, as well as some fishermen gathered together and organized the town. They chose the name Blocker's Bluff out of respect for the poor major's misfortune, and that's how the town got its name. They added Bluff because the far edge of the town was seven feet above sea level, so it seemed fitting to use the word bluff. They also elected the first mayor, a black man named Ezekiel Dickson.

The largest landholder was the Parker family. They had been in Blocker's Bluff since the mid-1800's and owned over thirty-five hundred acres of farmland west of town. The land was purchased from the State at little cost, since the State had no use for it, and needed money in its coffers after the Civil War. There was little flooding as the land had good drainage. The elder Mr. Parker also owned the small bank and the restaurant.

There wasn't much to the original town, just a general store, a livery stable and a covered pavilion that served as a place where the farmers and fishermen could barter or sell their goods. The pavilion was also a place where the men and their families could relax and enjoy good conversation over a roasted pig and moonshine for the men. Occasionally it served as the church when a traveling preacher came to town—which was a rare occurrence.

Today's town wasn't something you'd expect to see in the low country. It was something you'd expect to see further inland. There was no stoplight and no fast food outlets. There were one gas station, a restaurant and the local bank now owned by the original Parker's son. The only paved road is the one that goes through town. It's also the only way to get to the City of Crofton, I-95 and 174 providing access to Beaufort and Charleston.

Some one-lane dirt roads will get you there, but one can never tell if they flooded after a rainfall, especially in the low country. After Hurricane Hugo struck in 1989, all the roads flooded, and there was no exit from town to the inland.

The paved road was constructed by the Crofton County Utilities Cooperative—(CCUC) which supplies the needed electrical power. A few of the tiny towns within the county pooled their resources and formed the cooperative. CCUC's plant is located five miles outside the city of Crofton.

There's also no industry in Blocker's Bluff, and many of the townsfolk travel to Crofton, Beaufort or Charleston for employment. A few have found work at the CCUC plant.

At one point, the town had a doctor but, unfortunately, when Old Doc Elias, that's what folks called him, passed; no other physicians were interested in practicing medicine in a small rural town. Folks had to go to Crofton Regional Hospital in Crofton or travel to Beaufort or Charleston. There were doctors in Crofton County, but they wouldn't make house calls like Old Doc Elias did.

The local veterinarian, who also covered parts of the county, would do small things like stitches, some broken bones and sprains, but nothing major. There was no pharmacy either, but the general store carried some over-the-counter medications like aspirin and such.

A few vacant buildings in town were sometimes used as meeting places. In the event of a storm, the vacant buildings were used to store lumber and other necessities in preparation. Others housed small shops, the town jail, and police station.

Most of the townspeople were older and retired. It wasn't an ideal place to raise a family, but many had done so. Most of the young folk went off to one of the universities or colleges and tended not to return, or they moved to the city of Crofton. The College of Charleston, Clemson, and The Citadel were prime beneficiaries of the town's young people.

Blocker's Bluff never got caught up in the civil rights era, as most folks were too busy eking out a living to concern themselves with racial biases. Many of the older folk fought in WWII, and some lost sons and daughters in that war and Vietnam just like the Dicksons had lost their son, George. Many from Crofton enlisted after 9/11 and were in Afghanistan or Iraq.

The wars and a desire to stay alive kept the town folk pretty much united in their feelings toward one another. It made for a great place to grow up, unlike some parts of Crofton County.

Many who came from the inland cities and towns had bought or built houses there for use as weekend getaways. They came with their fishing boats and enjoyed great fishing. Blocker's Bluff had always been a first-rate fishing town.

Some of the townsfolk converted their homes to bed and breakfast inns, which enabled them to earn a little income. Most thrived off their small farms and bartered their crops in Crofton or at the local general store, which was owned by the mayor.

Parker's Restaurant had been the only eating establishment in Blocker's Bluff since 1940. The Parker family also owned the little bank that served the town and the restaurant. When Thomas Senior and his wife Rosalyn decided to retire to South Florida, their son Thomas Junior took over management of the restaurant and the bank in 1992.

The restaurant had six tables and a counter to eat on and served three meals a day. It also housed the post office and the general store. Breakfast was the busiest mealtime, and you could get a heaping helping of scrambled eggs with fresh baked biscuits or a giant stack of pancakes. The locals liked to spend mornings having breakfast and talking about almost anything just to have a place to congregate. You won't find better grits anywhere within five hundred miles. Lunchtime brought a decent crowd but at dinnertime, most of the locals ate at home.

Mayor Tom Parker had just finished breakfast, left the restaurant, and was confronted by a stranger. The Mayor seemed to recognize him and gave the guy an icy stare.

Chief of Police Molly Dickson had just left the restaurant and was walking toward her car when she overheard pieces of their conversation.

"You keep it up, and I'm going to tell your wife. For the sake of both of you, put a stop to it now!"

His comment got her attention. She waited before getting into her car and listened further.

Parker seemed upset, and his reply implied it.

"I'll stop when we're both ready to stop. Don't threaten me. You know damn well I can bring you down, and I damn well will do it!"

"You try it, and you go down too!" the stranger said and walked away.

Parker was in his mid-forties, lanky with a thinning hairline and a face that any mother might not love. His reputation was that he was a spoiled brat who never had to work for anything. Folks put up with him because he owned the only bank, restaurant and was the town's mayor.

His complexion was a shade whiter than before the confrontation. Chief Dickson thought about asking him but decided it was none of her business. As Chief of Police, unless it was breaking the law, she just minded her own business and let people do pretty much as they pleased.

Not much happened in Blocker's Bluff that required the need of a Chief of Police; nevertheless, the Town Council decided they wanted one. Molly liked the income, what little there was. But she was also a one-woman police force.

She wondered what that guy meant about telling Parker's wife. He had been married going on twenty years and had two kids in college. Parker and his wife seemed to have a good marriage but what she overheard sounded a little suspicious.

She just might ask John Porter when she visited him on his island for his opinion of Parker's conversation.

CHAPTER 2

Porter's Island was located just across the bay from Blocker's Bluff. It wasn't much of an island, mostly marshes but it served its purpose for the lone inhabitant. You could get there by boat in two hours, less if you had a fast one.

There were other small islands in other inlets, but most were uninhabited. Fishermen liked to use the waters around the islands to catch sea bass and other edible fish. Some of the men from Blocker's Bluff made a small living from their catches.

The island was named after the Porter family who brought it in the early 1900's from the state. There was nothing on the island except marshes until John Porter Senior built a large cabin on the south side of the island with the help of his son. It took them several years because they had to haul the materials by boat. Back then, all they had was a small johnboat with a rickety old outboard motor.

After Hurricane Hugo in 1989, Porter and his son visited the island to assess the storm damage. They cleared away debris, got what water was in the cabin out and made whatever repairs were necessary. Most of the damage was to the porch and the dock. With what little lumber they had, they made as many repairs as they could. After several return trips, they finally got the dock back to being serviceable. Without the dock, the cabin would be inhabitable. A year later they decided to move the cabin a little further inland and placed stilts under it in the event of future flooding. They also extended the dock. It was a difficult job, but they had help from two of Mr. Porter's friends and neighbors.

When the elder Porters died, they left the island and their home on the mainland to their son John Porter Junior—who was now the only occupant. Porter never liked the title of Junior. He was ready to fight anybody who called him Junior.

He took occupancy shortly after he retired as Chief of Police of Blocker's Bluff. He'd been living there going on five years and was practically a hermit. He didn't have a need for the house on the mainland, so he sold it and invested most of the funds with a financial advisor in Beaufort. Porter knew him from their military days. They had served together in Vietnam.

Porter had invested while he was Chief of Police and had a good amount in his portfolio. He also purchased an annuity, which provided him with periodic installments.

It's what he lived on. He didn't have much need for income while living on the Island.

He rarely went into town, and if it weren't for Molly Dickson visiting him, he'd be a modern day Robinson Crusoe.

When he moved into the cabin, he acquired a gas-powered generator that provided electricity to the cabin and also for the pump that provided running water, which had to be boiled before drinking, since it was sea-water. Two fifty-gallon gas drums fueled the generator. He gets the gas from a friend in Beaufort who periodically delivered new drums and took away the used ones.

Thanks to the running water, he was able to bathe every other day unless he'd been fishing. When that happened, he usually smelled of fish and the sea. If he didn't bathe, the dog wouldn't let him in the cabin. He shaved every other day, as he wanted to be sure he looked somewhat presentable for his favorite visitor.

His hair had gotten longer since he'd been on the island. When it got too long, he tied it in a ponytail until Molly visited and gave him a haircut. That happened about every four months.

He kept himself reasonably fit by taking long walks with his dog, Old George, and got additional exercise when he went fishing. Most of his exercise, however, was by tilting his arm when he drank his beer. Fortunately, he didn't show signs of a beer belly.

To his credit, he was careful about farting especially inside the cabin. When he did slip, Old George buried his head in his paws and whimpered. Of course, out on the porch, he didn't care since he figured the fresh air would dissipate the odor. Old George just got up and walked away leaving Porter with his smell. He was no dummy.

During Molly's occasional visits, he would accidentally let one slip and say his ass caught a cold and sneezed. Molly just shook her head. Then she and Old George would go outside. She was no dummy either.

Porter was just waking up and trying to get out of bed before company arrived. Old George was lying nearby watching him maneuver out of the bed. It was a struggle every morning, and he complained every time.

"Damn, it gets harder each day to get out this damn bed. You're lucky, Old George, you don't have to get up every day except to do your business and can sleep all day if you want to.

"I, on the other hand, have responsibilities although you don't think I do. That's because you're a dog, and I'm a human. We take care of our animals. Though you'd probably say you take care of me."

Old George had been Porter's dog since he was a pup twelve years ago. Porter named him after Molly's brother, his childhood buddy, who lost his life in the later years of the Vietnam War. George had less than a year left on his tour when he stepped on a mine and didn't make it back.

When Porter got the news, he was devastated. That's when his anger issues started. He survived the rest of his tour and came home, but you could tell he wasn't the same man who left Blocker's Bluff before being drafted.

"To hell with you, Old George! Hell, I'd better get the damn coffee made before that bitch gets here and nags me. She's worse than you. If I didn't know better, I'd swear you're bred from her. That sounds like her boat now." Old George ignored him. "Any minute she'll yell, 'Hey old man come and help me!' Well, she can just wait till the coffee's made and I'm dressed."

As her boat pulled up to the rickety old dock, Molly cursed because Porter had been living on the island long enough to have made major repairs to it by now.

It's a wonder neither of them had fallen through the damn thing. Molly secured the boat then disembarked, careful not to fall. She often asked why she made the trip here, especially since her boat wasn't much bigger than a johnboat.

It did have a good running outboard motor; otherwise, the trip would be near impossible. Porter kept telling her she needed a bigger boat but, like him, she was stubborn and always said, "Hell no!"

Molly became Chief of Police when Porter retired or, rather, was forced to retire. He had a severe anger issue. Whenever things didn't go his way, he managed to piss off some townsfolk until the Town Council finally had enough and asked him to retire after twenty-five years as the chief.

The Town Council was comprised equally of white and black members. It was the Mayor, Tom Parker, and the white members who forced him to retire. Porter and Parker never liked each other and after that, even more so.

Porter didn't go away quickly. He smashed the only patrol car the town owned and left the chief's office in a mess. The Town Council decided not to press charges, as they just wanted him gone. They gave him a small severance package and wished him well.

Molly was unanimously elected as the new Chief of Police, probably because no one else would take the job. It also helped that she was a black female. The pay was next to nothing, and the benefits were the same except she got free meals at Parker's Restaurant. The Mayor owned the restaurant so it was a convenient benefit to give.

Molly wasn't new to law enforcement. After getting a degree in Criminal Justice from the College of Charleston, the South Carolina Highway Patrol hired her and based her out of Beaufort, which was convenient since she still lived with her parents. After twenty-one years and with the rank of Sergeant, she took a hardship retirement to care for her parents who were severely ill. After they both had passed, Molly inherited the house and had lived there since.

She kept herself reasonably fit with daily exercise, was still attractive, often complimented on her looks, especially by Porter, and wore her uniform well.

Both had reached the mid-century mark. Neither showed their age. To most folks, they seemed ten years younger, but if you ever saw Porter getting out of bed, you'd swear he was pushing seventy.

They'd known each ever since high school. The high school was long gone, and now the kids are bused or drive their pickup trucks to the schools in Crofton. Pickups had become the standard means of transportation for most folks young and old.

Porter and Molly almost got hitched, but she got cold feet at the last minute. She just didn't feel he was the marrying kind, and there was the racial thing. Her parents weren't too keen on them being the first biracial marriage in South Carolina. They've been good friends ever since.

"Hey, old man! Get your lazy ass out here and help me, or I'll leave these provisions on the dock where they'll rot waiting for you to come get them!"

"Hold your damn britches, you old bitch. I'm coming, and who the hell you calling old man?"

"You! Who did you think I was talking to, Old George there? He's got more life in him than you do. I don't know why the hell I come here."

"You come for the sex that's why, and don't deny it!"

"You call that sex? If you keep talking and don't get down here, the only sex you're gonna get is from that arthritic hand of yours. Now get your ass over here!"

That was how most of their conversations went, but it was also how they expressed their feelings. They sure cared for each other, but just wouldn't admit it.

"Alright already! You know, it's either my eyesight is getting bad or the sun's blinding me, but you look exceptionally good this morning."

He loved to flatter her and always hoped that it would get her into his bed. Sometimes it worked and sometimes it didn't, but he kept trying.

"Never mind the phony flattery. You just want me to go to bed with you in that thing you call a bed. When's the last time you bought a new mattress?"

"If a new mattress is all it takes, next time you come back bring me a new one. We can christen it together."

Old George was enjoying the banter between the two of them. If he could speak like a human, he would laugh out loud, but instead rolled over and feigned disinterest.

"You'll never change! Take these. I hope that's coffee I smell and not your dirty socks!"

"Ready and waiting for you, my fair princess."

"Fair princess, my ass!"

"I love it when you talk dirty."

`He did indeed love it when she spoke what he called dirty. It was how he knew she cared about him.

"Let's go; I got something important to talk to you about."

"What, the Town Council wants me back as Chief of Police?"

Porter knew that was never going to happen but liked mentioning it as often as he could. Molly always had the same response. They were beginning to sound like old married folk. Anyone who heard the way they talked to each other would swear they were.

"When hell freezes over. Come on. I need coffee."

"At your beck and call!"

She gave him her usual sarcastic look then continued.

Porter just smiled as always.

Old George covered his head with his paws.

CHAPTER 3

The inside of Porter's cabin wasn't much better than the outside including the dock. It needed more than a woman's touch, it would take an entire army of women and a brigade of carpenters to spruce it up. It looked like a Saturday morning garage sale.

There was so much stuff scattered around. Most of it was usable, but Porter hadn't bothered to stow it away or use any of it since he moved back into the cabin. Molly had often offered to help him clean up the mess, but he always told her to leave it, he'd get to it eventually.

John Porter had never been one to take care of himself, nor anything he owned. He smacked his last pickup truck into a tree and almost killed himself. Porter said the damn tree got in his way. That's the way he'd been ever since Molly first met him. Now he relied on Molly to drive him, if need be.

In high school, he was a great linebacker because he could break through any offensive line put in front of him. The only problem was that he was off sides more times than not—which was why the school lost so many games—all due to excessive penalties. One team almost scored a touchdown on his penalties alone.

"Porter, you know if it weren't for me bringing you supplies every other week, you dumb son of a bitch, you'd starve to death. It's a wonder you even wipes your ass."

Molly knew he at least bathes, even if it was just a swim in the bay. The honest truth was that she loved the old bastard—had ever since she first met him.

She would have married him that one time if she could have been sure he could control his anger. He wasn't the same after George died in Vietnam. She did what she thought was best for her.

Porter ignored her comment as always and replied, "What is it you want to talk to me about?"

"First off, I saw that fancy boat go by heading to the other side of the island again. Wonder what they're doing over there?"

She'd seen that boat several times and each time she got more curious. It was starting to gnaw at her gut. Porter never thought it was anything to be concerned about.

"May not be doing anything. Ain't nothing over there 'cept groves, and you can't put up a structure without getting my okay. And nobody's asked me for permission. Probably fishing or swimming bare-ass. What else is up?"

Molly was curious as to what he would think about Parker's conversation with the stranger. Maybe he'd have some insight; after all he used to be the Chief of Police.

"Yesterday after breakfast as I was leaving Parker's Restaurant, this guy got in Parker's face. The Mayor didn't look too happy about whatever they were talking about because his face got all red. I'd say he looked a little unnerved after the guy left."

She thought he might comment but he just listened. "Couldn't tell who the guy was, never seen him around town. The Mayor's been going out of town an awful lot the past six months. Never says what for. You got any thoughts?"

Porter had no clue as to what it was all about and didn't care as long everyone damn well left him alone. Since he was practically a hermit on his island, what would he know about what the Mayor was up to—cept he liked making conversation with Molly.

"I'd say if he looked unnerved, then the Mayor must be up to something when he makes those trips. Maybe you should see if you could find out where he goes. Could be something, could be nothing. Anyway, you know I don't really care much about what Parker does. Is that it?"

"Yes, but I'm just curious. It's my nature. And speaking of nature, is that bathroom of yours clean or am I gonna have to go out back again?"

"I cleaned it yesterday. Ask Old George, if you don't believe me, check it out yourself."

"I'm afraid to look, but I got to go bad."

It was a bathroom, but it was more like an indoor outhouse. Molly checked and damn if it wasn't clean enough to use. Even the odor was slightly fresh. He must have really done a job cleaning it so she decided to use it.

"See, what did I tell you? Is that good enough to get you to stay the night? I've been missing you Molly, an awful lot!"

"Okay, this time I can stay. Ain't like anything's gonna happen in town that needs the Chief of Police. Just make sure you're a good boy."

"I always am, it's just that you still make my heart flutter!"

She stayed the night, and he was good just like he always was, and she was glad to be with him. He still took her breath away and the old bastard could make her cry out with pleasure.

It's why she still loved him. He got satisfaction, and she got pleasure. It was a good trade off.

CHAPTER 4

Atlanta, Georgia

In her townhouse, Melanie Tifton and her brother, Johnny, were discussing his recent trip to Blocker's Bluff. They lived together, and she'd been looking out for him ever since their parents died.

"I talked to Parker, and he's not going to back off. He said he'd stop when you want him to. This thing is getting out of hand, and you've got to do something!"

His comment annoyed her. "I'll take care of Parker. You need to back off! I know what I'm doing. He's just a hick town Mayor going through a midlife crisis, and hasn't got a clue what's going on."

"If you say so, but we've been in this situation before, and it didn't go well."

He was right; there had been several times and things did go wrong—which was why he was concerned.

"That's because we brought McPayne in on the action, and he screwed everything up. We don't have to worry about him this time, Johnny."

"Yes, but what if somehow he gets wind of what we're doing?"

"If that happens we'll deal with it then. Now stay away from Parker!"

She often asked herself why she let Johnny in on her schemes. He worried too much, and if she weren't his sister watching over him, he'd probably be in jail.

Their mother and father spoiled him just because he had an adverse reaction to a Smallpox vaccination.

Johnny barely got through high school and couldn't keep a job while she worked her way through college. She never had a real chance to put her art degree to good use.

Melanie came close to marriage once, but the guy turned out to be a chronic cheater.

She ran her first scam just out of college as a means of paying off her student loans. Nobody would ever say Melanie Stevens was dumb.

CHAPTER 5

Growing up in Greenwood, South Carolina wasn't all that bad for the Stevens children. At least they were brought up by both their parents unlike some of their friends who were raised by a single parent or by grandparents.

The family lived in a small bungalow with three bedrooms, which was good because she sure didn't want to share a bedroom with her brother Billy. One thing for certain, they didn't live in an affluent neighborhood. Both of their parents worked and did everything they could to assure them of a decent home life.

Billy had many issues, and their mother and father babied him. When they passed away, they left his sister with the responsibility of caring for him. He was five years younger than her. Fortunately, she had already graduated from college at the time.

Melanie was pushing thirty-six now and working on her third big scam. Her first one was shortly after graduating from Tramin University in Greenwood. She had a sizable amount of student loan debt to pay off and needed to make some big money quick.

In college, she managed to keep her expenses down by rooming with another art major. It was a good pairing, and they got along well since they had something in common.

Back then, her name was Debbie Stevens. Since then, she'd had a few other names until she became Melanie Tifton.

Her art degree wasn't much help in finding decent paying jobs, especially in Greenwood and Columbia, so she tried Atlanta. She was able to land a few jobs, but nothing that paid the kind of money she needed.

She met Bill McPayne at a job fair. They started talking and seemed to hit it off, so she went out with him a few times. She thought he was kind of bright and had some good ideas.

They were going together for quite some time, and she thought he loved her. She wasn't a virgin when she met him, and he certainly was good in bed. That's where she made her mistake.

McPayne told her he had this plan to make money by selling penny stocks. He wanted her to be his administrative assistant and greet potential customers when they came to his office.

An office wasn't an accurate description of his operation. What he had were some empty spaces to make it look like he had a fair size operation with a number of brokers using private offices. The prospect couldn't tell it was a one-man operation.

He wanted her good looks and attractive figure to lure men into investing. She always wore short skirts and low cut tops making sure the men had a good look.

It worked for two years until the markets took a tumble, leaving some unhappy investors who found out their penny stocks were worth just that, one penny.

One thing she was good at was creating fake identification; that's where her background in art came in handy. She maintained a cache of forged identification papers including driver's licenses and such.

McPayne closed up shop and left Atlanta. She never saw him again until several years later.

At the time, her name was Candy Thomas, so she was able to move on to a job as a department store clerk using the name Mandy Perkins.

That job lasted a whole year; long enough to make enough to get her back on her feet. That's when she decided to try her hand at the con game. She started small with something she knew, which was art. No forgeries and no stolen art.

Mandy Perkins could draw and paint, so she made reproductions and sold them as originals. She stuck to high-end art shows, and her work did well. Next, she expanded her market and soon was getting orders for more than she could handle and had to mass-produce.

She didn't have the resources or equipment to handle the volume and looked for a partner. Her brother was willing to help, but she needed more. That's when Bill McPayne came back into the picture.

He had the ability to put together the type of operation she wanted, so Mandy made the mistake of letting him in as a partner. The problem was she didn't find out soon enough that he was pulling a scam on her.

She had the orders, and he decided they needed the buyers to front load their purchases. When they had a good number of deposits that amounted to five figures, McPayne took off with the money. Mandy made the mistake of letting him handle the money.

He was supposed to use it for reproducing the artwork. Fortunately, Mandy Perkins was another fictitious name. She also used a disguise so her real identity wouldn't be part of the scam, but she had to make a bunch of apologies and leave Atlanta for a year. She returned as Melanie Tifton. Her brother became Johnny Tifton thanks to Melanie's talents.

The thing with Tom Parker could be big for her and Johnny if Parker didn't mess it up.

The problem was Parker thought he was in love with her and kept coming to Atlanta. She'd been able to keep him involved by sleeping with him each time. Unfortunately, that's why he had come to think he was in love with her. Maybe his wife didn't give him enough, and he'd been starving for gratification. Whatever the reason, Melanie needed him.

She also has the threat of infidelity to use if need be. It would be new for her, but she was determined to see the scam through. Johnny was still her weakest link, but she believed she could control him too.

CHAPTER 6

The Parkers lived in the only affluent neighborhood in Blocker's Bluff. There were only five houses in the neighborhood, and each sat on a half-acre of property.

One of the local youth, who was attending the College of Charleston, mowed the lawn and freshened up the landscape for the Mayor. He came home every other weekend, and what Parker paid him, he used as date money.

Their house and property were the largest since it was the Mayor's residence. The house originally belonged to Parker's parents. When they retired and moved away, they gave it to Parker and his wife.

Barbara Parker was visibly upset. Her husband had been acting suspicious for quite some time, and she wanted to know why. It wasn't like him to keep secrets from her.

She thought they had a good marriage, but he'd been avoiding her in the bedroom. Every time she tried to engage him in conversation he just brushed her off. It had been wearing on her both physically and emotionally.

They were both standing in the kitchen. Parker was pouring himself a drink when Barbara decided to try again.

"Tom, you have to tell me what's going on? Why are you making so many trips to Atlanta?"

"Barbara, nothing is going on. I have some business there, and you need not concern yourself!"

It was the same response he always gave her each time she inquired. She seriously doubted what he told her. Even the look on his face was enough to tell her he was hiding something.

"I don't believe you, Tom. You're not telling me the truth. Are you seeing someone in Atlanta or are you getting yourself into something that's going to bring trouble to our family?"

"Please, Barbara, it's nothing. Don't be foolish. Why would I want to have an affair?" He smiled. "Don't you know how much I love you and the kids? Can't you just let it rest and trust me for once?"

Trust him? How could she when he was so secretive?

"I've always trusted you, but something tells me there's more to your trips then you're telling me. I know you, and you've never been as secretive as you've been this past year. I want to know what's going on!"

He took a sip of his drink and frowned. "Just forget it, Barbara. I'm going to the bank. I'll see you for dinner."

Once again he was dismissing her, and she was tired of it. She was going to do something. If he wasn't willing to be forthright with her, she was going to let him know.

"Tom, we're not finished. I'm going to find out what's going on. One way or the other."

Parker stormed out of the house and left. Barbara had terribly upset him, and he was afraid she might interfere and destroy his plans. Parker couldn't let that happen, and would have to tell Melanie about the incident.

Barbara was thoroughly annoying him, which was one reason he started shunning her in the bedroom. But she also wasn't accommodating his needs, and this was important to him.

He didn't know what he was going to do. Maybe he shouldn't tell Melanie. She might get upset, and that brother of hers could make trouble. Next time he's in Atlanta, he'll approach Melanie and see what she thought.

At least she was more reasonable than her brother. Nothing was going to get in the way of his plans.

"If only Barbara wasn't so damn inquisitive all the time. Once she gets her teeth into something, she doesn't let go of it," he said to himself.

Parker seemed to have one problem after another popping up. His plans were getting more and more difficult.

CHAPTER 7

A year earlier in Atlanta, Tom Parker was sitting at the hotel bar nursing a drink. He'd been there for quite some time and wished he had stayed home. The Mayor's convention was proving to be a waste of his day, and Parker wished he hadn't come. At least he only had one more night before he would leave Atlanta. If only he knew where to find some action.

It's not that he didn't love Barbara, but lately, she'd become too much of a damn Southern Bell and sex with her was like having it by himself. He told himself he had needs, and a wife shouldn't hold back.

An attractive brunette noticed him and walked over and sat down next to him. The woman was wearing a very short and very tight dress that gave him an excellent view of her legs, which he had trouble taking his eyes off. He managed to do so because her top also revealed a gorgeous view of her well-rounded breasts. Parker thought that maybe he'd found some action after all.

"Hi, my name is Melanie. What's yours?"

"And hi back to you! My name's Tom. Pleased to meet you, Melanie."

His mind immediately wandered to his hotel room with her in it with him. Could he be this lucky? He fancied himself a ladies man and believed he could charm most women, especially when dressed in business attire. Back home, he was the only man who wore a suit and tie.

"You look bored, Tom. Are you here on business or do you live in Atlanta?"

Tom's eyes immediately went to her shapely legs and another quick gaze at her chest. He suddenly felt a sensation between his legs.

"I'm bored all right but, no, I don't live in Atlanta. I'm here for a Mayor's Conference, and it was the biggest mistake I ever made coming. Are you from Atlanta?"

She noticed where his eyes were focused and purposely leaned forward.

"Yes, I am. What made you come to the conference?"

"I was hoping to make some contacts for a real estate project I'm considering putting together."

Sounded like a good line, he thought, and there was some truth to it. That sensation between his legs was growing more intense, and so was his imagination.

Melanie suddenly saw visions of dollar signs in her head. She tilted her head and leaned in again as though listening with more intent. Melanie needed another new deal and new mark, and he might just be the one.

"Well Tom, I'm very familiar with real estate projects. Why don't you tell me about it? Does it involve land sales?"

"No, not property sales. I own just over 3,500 acres near the South Carolina coast, and I want to put together a combination resort and housing community, but I need backing."

"I may be able to help you there. I've put together some such packages and have many contacts. Why don't we sit at a table, and you can tell me more if that's okay with you?"

Of course, that wasn't true, but Melanie was baiting her mark—the way she always did.

Parker was never one to turn down a good-looking woman, and Melanie sure was a looker. He decided he could use some advice and maybe even a little something else. Why not? He told himself. What did he have to lose?

"Sure. Let's do that."

They sat at a table, and he ordered a round of drinks then he told her all about his idea. She seemed interested and said she wanted to know more. He told her the land had been in his family for several generations and that he also owned the local bank.

Melanie could feel the excitement. Christmas was coming early for her.

"Then you have access to funds, Tom. Am I right?"

"Technically, no, but if necessary, I can get my hands on some. Why, do you think I'm going to need some upfront money?"

She found her hook and went for it. Tonight, she'd entice Parker when they're together. It's what she'd always been good at doing. Bait the hook with sex then reel them in.

"You're going to need some seed money if you want investors to believe you're for real. How much can you get initially?"

"Would $15,000 do it?"

It was good enough to start, but she was sure she could get more out of him. She was hoping for a nice six-figure deal. The guy seemed clueless.

"It's a start, but you'll need more pretty quick. Tell you what; I'm bored with this place. Why don't we go someplace else and talk some more? Do you have a hotel room we can use?"

Parker couldn't believe what she'd just asked. Was he going to get her to his hotel room? How lucky could he be?

"Sure, it has a good size seating area, and we can use the mini bar. That way we don't have to order from room service if that's okay with you? I don't want you to think I'm suggesting anything improper."

You're not she told herself, but I am.

"Tom, I've been down this road before. I know what it takes to make a business deal." She reached for his hand. "Come on, let's get out of here."

Melanie was thinking, boy this guy is clueless and has a bulge in his pants already. If the mere mention of going to his room excited him so much, just think what she could get him to do when they're in bed. If necessary, she would do whatever was needed tonight to get her the 15K and more after that.

Parker's heart pounded from excitement. He couldn't believe that she accepted his offer. Sparks were flying between his legs. He told himself that whether or not she could help, he was going to make a play for her. He would probably never see her again, so why not. If she was for real, so be it.

When he stood, he had to be careful because that sensation became more than just an arousal, and he didn't want her to notice the bulge in his pants.

In the hotel room, Tom told Melanie more about his plan. She said she could get the necessary prospectuses put together, but would need the money very soon before going forward.

"I can get the $15,000 rather quickly if need be. When I do, you think we can get together soon after?"

"I don't see why not."

They both agreed to another meeting and shook hands saying they were partners. They would formalize it the next time they saw each other.

He thought to himself, why not go for something more? If she says yes, then the night would be well spent. If not, nothing's lost as he was going to spend the night alone regardless.

"Do you have to go, Melanie?"

"I can stay, Tom, if you'd like?" She winked at him.

"I would. Why don't I fix us a drink?"

Parker was so excited that he almost made a fool of himself. But he managed to stay in control. After sharing a few drinks, she suggested they retire to the bed.

Melanie was surprisingly good, and he got what he'd wanted from his wife ever since they were married. It was the most exciting experience he'd ever had and soon after fell asleep. He even had a wet dream about her.

The next morning, Tom and Melanie shook hands and said they would meet in his hotel room again next time, formalize their partnership, and then meet up at her office. She gave him a card with her telephone number and said next time she would have proper business cards for him.

She left the hotel thinking how easy it was to satisfy Parker, and he even had a wet dream after what she did to him. Melanie was going to milk this one even if she had to keep satisfying the moron.

Tom was so excited and felt things were going to work out, but he wouldn't say anything to anyone until everything was in place. He went to the conference and afterward went back to Blocker's Bluff.

Two weeks later, he met Melanie and gave her the money. After the finances were taken care of he asked if she would spend the night.

She gave him her most provocative smile, said yes and then led him to the bed.

Melanie was pretty good in bed, but he was more interested in something other than intercourse. It wasn't what she preferred, but if that's what it took to satisfy him, what the hell. She'd done it before with other men.

In the morning, they finalized their partnership. Melanie gave him some cards with her office number and address.

Before he went home, she told him she needed more for the prospectuses.

"How much more?"

"Another 15K. But we'll need fifty more after that."

"I'll have the fifteen next time we get together."

To seal the deal, she kissed him and then he left.

Melanie was pleased with herself. She used the money to put a deposit on a small office and had business cards printed.

It was going to be a different experience for Melanie, as she'd never had to provide so many sexual favors to satisfy a mark. But there was always a first time, especially if it got her $50,000 and possibly more.

CHAPTER 8

The Bank of Blocker's Bluff was so small that it wasn't even considered a community bank by banking standards. The bank was usually never crowded. The interior furnishings were modest with a nice seating area. The décor was a bit old fashioned and stodgy looking but it worked because customers only spent a little time inside, there was no drive-up window as there was no need.

Most of the townsfolk did their banking a few times a week, mostly in the afternoon. Mornings were spent taking care of official business and processing what few loan applications there were.

Linda Jacobs, the bank manager, was always the first to arrive. The two tellers came in at nine o'clock since the bank's hours were from nine thirty to four. Most banks in South Carolina opened at nine and closed at five, but The Bank of Blocker's Bluff still clung to its old ways. There was no need to open earlier or close later.

Linda was already in when Tom Parker arrived at 8:15. She greeted him as she did every morning.

"Good morning, Mr. Parker! Is everything okay?"

"Yes, Linda, everything's okay. Why do you ask?"

"Well, you looked a little annoyed when you came in."

"It's nothing, just a little annoyance at home. I spilled coffee on the floor, and Barbara got irritated." It sounded like a good excuse. "Honestly, I don't know why it was such a big deal. Are all women like that?"

"Can't say. I know I'm not." She smiled and added, "Can I do anything to calm your nerves? I'd be happy to."

"You always seem to know what I need. Do we have time for a shoulder massage before the others arrive?"

"There's plenty of time, and I'd be glad to do it. Why don't we go into your office?"

"Okay, but close the door. I don't want anyone walking in on us."

Linda had worked for Parker the past four years. She was a single woman who never married, and secretly had a crush on Parker when they were in high school. When he married Barbara, she was disappointed and moved away. She worked for several banks until he hired her after a chance meeting at an ABA Conference.

The two of them had been meeting secretly in his office for several years. Linda was satisfied with their arrangement and knew he was taking advantage of her. But she was the one who initiated things before Parker hired her.

When they finished, Linda got up off the floor and asked how things were going in Atlanta. Tom hadn't said anything about Atlanta, but Linda knew he had been making several trips there.

Parker knew that eventually he'd have to confide in Linda if this deal was going to succeed. He'd need her help because he would have to use more bank funds for the next phase.

He'd already used $15,000 and any more would require significant precautions—which was why he needed her. For now, he'd leave things as they were. He zipped his pants, buckled his belt, and was ready to respond. But his breathing was a little rapid, so he hesitated to allow for a calm inflection.

"So far things are going okay. Soon I'll tell you more as I'm going to need your help and advice."

"Whenever you're ready, Tom. You know I'm always here for you!"

Exactly what he wanted to hear.

CHAPTER 9

Barbara's best friend and confidant was Judy Waverly. They've been longtime friends since high school. They were both cheerleaders. Judy was divorced with two grown kids in college. Her ex pays their tuition.

Judy still lived in her parents' house. She moved there after the divorce and lived with her father until he passed away in 2003. Judy was the same age as Barbara and always dressed professionally in white blouses and knee-length skirts—the same as before the divorce. Her hair was brown and cut short, the way she liked it.

She was the only realtor in Blocker's Bluff. Real estate sales were not that extensive, so she had lots of time on her hands. She made enough from sales to be self-sufficient.

When Barbara called and said she wanted to talk with her, Judy had an idea what it probably was. Barbara had mentioned on several occasions that she suspected her husband was up to something. His trips to Atlanta once a month had made her suspicious.

Judy knew what it was like to have a cheating spouse, as that's what broke up her marriage. If Tom Parker were having an affair, then she would be there for her friend. Barbara was there for her every time she needed one.

When Barbara arrived the first thing she said was, "I need a glass of wine, now! I'd ask for something stronger but it's too early, and I don't want to get drunk!"

Judy poured them both a glass of wine and sat down next to her. "Why are you so upset? Are you going to fill me in on everything this time?"

"You bet. That SOB told me nothing was going on and just to forget it! Forget it! I can't because he keeps saying he has business in Atlanta but won't say what. What kind of business could he have in Atlanta? He's the mayor of a small town, owner of its only restaurant, and owner of a tiny bank. It's all bullshit!"

"So, what are you going to do? Do you want to go to Atlanta and spy on him? If you do, I'm up for a road trip."

Judy could use a little excitement and a trip to Atlanta would be fun, especially if it meant spying on Parker. She never liked him but never told Barbara.

"I'm seriously considering doing just that. I'd hire a private investigator, but I don't know any. I'd even consider talking to John Porter. He'd love to get payback for what Tom and the Town Council did that screwed him over royally."

"You know what, Barbara? I think that would be a good idea. But we'll need a subtle way to approach him. Have another glass of wine, and we'll think about it."

Judy poured them each another glass of wine, and they tossed some ideas around, but none seemed doable.

"I wonder if Linda could shed any light on his trips to Atlanta."

"I don't know, Barbara, she's too close to Tom and has been with him so long. She may be protective of him, especially if it has something to do with the bank. I would put that thought aside for now."

"You're right. Besides, Linda's had a crush on Tom ever since high school. Here's a thought! What if Tom is having an affair with Linda? Wouldn't that be something?"

"I don't think he's Linda's type. Linda was always different from the rest of us. I mean, she was our friend, but there was something a little strange about her. I think you're way off base about Tom and Linda."

"You're probably right. Let's forget Linda."

Judy was pleased that Barbara decided not to pursue the Linda and Tom possibility. She liked Linda and was glad she was back in town. She and Linda occasionally got together for girl talk.

"Well, it looks like we're either going to Atlanta ourselves, or we'll have to find a way to speak with John Porter. I'd suggest talking to Molly about it, but she's the Chief of Police, and I don't want her involved."

"Let it rest for now until we come up with a solution, or are you hell bent on going to Atlanta?"

"I'll let it rest for now. Besides, I wouldn't know how to go about following Tom in Atlanta. I'll need a good plan."

They let it be for now, and Barbara seemed much calmer than when she first arrived. After a while, Barbara went home, and Judy dressed to go out and meet with someone special.

CHAPTER 10

Charlotte, North Carolina—1999

Tom Parker had come to the American Bankers Conference just to get away from Blocker's Bluff and for a little relaxation. He was sitting alone at the hotel bar considering what he'd do that evening. Parker wasn't interested in hooking up with any of the other bankers at the Conference. He had nothing in common with them since most were from large regional banks.

He was nursing his second drink when suddenly an attractive looking woman approached him dressed in business attire, with an excellent figure, and great legs—which he was admiring. They were always the first place his eyes focused on before gravitating to above the waist. The woman's face looked vaguely familiar.

"Tom Parker? Is that you? What brings you to Charlotte?"

"Linda Jacobs! It is you. I'm here for the ABA Conference. What are you doing here?"

He couldn't believe how lovely she was. Parker wasn't sure how long it had been since he last saw her. It was probably around the time he married Barbara. The woman he was looking at was much more alluring than Barbara was in every way.

"I'm here for the Conference too. Are you still running the bank in Blocker's Bluff?"

"Yes, and I'm looking for a manager if you know of one?"

"I've been the branch manager at Second Union for the past five years. It's an okay bank to work for, but banking is not what it used to be now that the large banks have gobbled up all the community banks. Too much bureaucracy and politics for me. I like the way it used to be."

"There's no bureaucracy at my bank, just me if you want a change?"

Linda's mind started working. His offer was good news for her because she needed a change and a position far from where she was now employed. Parker didn't need to know all the details.

"I just might take you up on your offer. How are Barbara and the kids? You two still married?"

"Still married, and Barbara and the kids are fine. So tell me what you have been up to besides banking. Are you married?"

"Nope! I never got over my crush on you!"

"I didn't know you had one."

She didn't but it sounded like a good way to keep him interested in her.

"Oh, yes, ever since high school. When you married Barbara, that's when I decided there was no chance for me, so I left Blocker's Bluff. You broke my heart, Tom!"

"I didn't know that, Linda. I'm sorry."

He always was gullible. "Don't be. I got over it but not you. You want to get together for a drink tonight after the Conference?"

Tom was pleasantly surprised that she still had feelings for him, maybe there was more. Why not find out? The Conference may just have become worth his while, at least he hoped so.

"Sure, why not? How about we meet in the hotel lounge?"

He got up slowly so as not to embarrass himself.

"Great! I'll see you around seven. Don't disappoint me, Tom."

She had more than just a drink planned, and he was thinking the same thing. Here they were in Charlotte, far enough away from home. Parker's biggest weakness always was that he couldn't keep his pecker in his pants.

The slightest hint from a woman and he was ready to unzip his trousers, and Linda seemed like she was hinting at more than a drink.

He didn't disappoint Linda that night, and they did much more than just share a drink. Linda wanted a chance at the bank manager's position and was willing to fulfill his needs. She knew just what to do to satisfy him. Nothing had changed with Tom Parker. A BJ still did it for him.

In high school, when most guys were getting laid, Parker looked for girls who liked to put their head in his lap. The ones who did didn't mind because he had the fanciest car, always had plenty of money for a great date, and they enjoyed the places he took them—which were far away from Crofton County. Parker went through almost the entire cheerleading squad except for Judy Waverly and her best friend, Miss Goody two shoes, Barbara Millston. He still hadn't gotten one from her even though he married her.

There was nothing special about Parker in bed; he was barely adequate. Certainly not like that special someone back in Blocker's Bluff she was hoping to make a connection.

In the morning, they went to breakfast together. Both had smiles on their faces. The night before proved to be something they both wanted.

She asked Tom if she could send him her resume, and he said yes, but he could do without it. She said he must have a resume because if she goes to work for him, the Bank Examiners would want to see that Parker duly hired her. He would even have to do the necessary background check.

Linda didn't care about the salary. It wasn't about the money. She had other agendas that included Tom and renewing a close friendship with someone else from high school.

Within six months, Linda was the new bank manager, with everything properly handled. Even Barbara was amazed at her credentials. She told Tom she wasn't aware Linda had such an extensive banking career.

Within a year, Tom and Linda started doing their little thing twice a week before opening the bank. Parker got what he wanted, and Linda was happy to oblige. She had found other pleasures with someone special. They were very discreet so as not let the tellers know or have Barbara suspect anything.

As far as Linda was concerned, she had a job as long as he owned the bank and a lover for as long as she wanted. She also had renewed a very close friendship with someone else.

CHAPTER 11

The Blocker's Bluff' Police Department was nothing like those of most small towns in South Carolina. It was a small, unused office building with two rooms and a bathroom. One room served as the Chief's office. The other room was the jail for the random townsfolk who imbibed too much and needed a place to sleep it off—instead of driving home and getting into an accident.

A cell door was installed a long time ago by John Porter. There was also a small cot that Molly used when she worked an all-nighter. Porter used it more often as he practically lived there after his parents died, and he had sold their house.

Molly was more concerned about events concerning Parker, didn't like what was going on with him. Something wasn't right.

Porter didn't think it was anything she should concern herself with, but Molly just couldn't help her nagging suspicions. Whatever it was, somehow she'd figure it out with or without Porter's help—which she always did.

That fancy boat she kept seeing whenever she visited Porter was yet another thing that had her suspicious. She'd follow it, but her boat would never keep up with it. Somehow she would get to the bottom of what it was about.

Porter's boat was faster, but he wouldn't think there was anything to be concerned. He never thought there was anything to just about everything.

Molly wondered how she could get him interested in what's going on in town, but all he cared about was his life on Porter's Island. He never got over being forced out as chief and was still pissed at Parker and the Town Council.

While she was pondering what to do about Porter, she noticed Linda Jacobs was closing the bank and leaving at an unusually early hour. Linda frequently worked late and didn't leave until after Parker.

Maybe Parker was on one of his trips. She wondered what he did on those trips. Bet Porter could find out if only she could get him interested.

Since nothing was happening, she decided to close up early and go to Parker's Restaurant for an early dinner. For some reason, she didn't feel like cooking or eating alone. Damn, she sure hoped Porter wasn't wearing on her.

"Well, would you look at that?" Molly exclaimed. "What's Barbara doing in town? She rarely comes in by herself, and she's headed to the bank. Too bad, because she missed Jacobs."

Molly decided to watch and see what Barbara did.

"That's strange; Barbara looked pissed that nobody was there. She should have called if she wanted to talk to Jacobs unless she was looking for Parker."

Barbara seemed to be heading home. Molly would have stopped her and asked what was wrong but didn't want to get involved with something that didn't concern her. If she and Parker were having trouble, it was none of her business as long as they weren't breaking the law.

Molly was hungry and wasn't interested in anything else stopping her from getting to Parker's Restaurant for dinner. She knew Chef Willie would be serving up something good as he always did. She enjoyed visiting him, although it wasn't often enough.

CHAPTER 12

When Molly entered the restaurant, Chef Willie immediately greeted her. He was always happy to see her.

"Hey, Chief Molly! How you doing?"

The aroma of his cooking filled her nostrils and made her realize just how hungry she was for some good Southern home cooking. She was the only customer since it was dinner time and most folks ate at home—except for a few fishermen who occasionally stopped in before going out for an evening of fishing.

"Okay, Chef Willie! How's Miss Mavis, and what's for dinner today?"

"Miss Mavis is fine. She's busy washing dishes. I'll tell her you're here. You doing me the honor of letting me cook for you? How about catfish and taters?"

She could never resist his catfish and taters. It's what she grew up on and never outgrew them. Plus, Chef Willie made the best for miles around.

"Sounds good to me! Anything new going on that you know of?"

"Like what?"

"Oh, I don't know. What's your boss up to with his trips to Atlanta?"

If anyone knew something, it would be Chef Willie. Even though Parker was his boss, he knew nothing about running the restaurant. Without Chef Willie, the restaurant couldn't exist.

"Don't know, Chief. He don't confide in me, but he sure makes a lot of them. If it weren't for Linda being the bank manager, I'd be concerned. She knows more about running a bank than he will ever know."

Just like Chef Willie knew more about running a restaurant than Parker.

"Can't say I disagree with you, but you best keep that to yourself."

He smiled and waved his hand. "Sit down. Catfish and taters coming up for my favorite Chief of Police."

Willie was sixty years old and had been the chef at Parker's Restaurant nearly two decades. He was a chef in the Army and retired after twenty years' service. His wife Mavis had also retired from the military. They both collect a small pension.

Folks from around here didn't consider Willie as black same as they didn't think of Molly as black. That's the way it had always been here.

Mavis ran the restaurant's small bakery as well as the post office and general store. She baked bread, pies, and muffins for the restaurant and the general store. Mavis also helped with washing dishes after she closed up the general store. Willie makes the biscuits.

Chef Willie and Mavis lived in a small bungalow out behind the restaurant that was built by Mr. Parker Senior, specifically for them. Considering the hours they worked, it made it convenient for them. They also paid no rent as part of their employment agreement, but they were responsible for utilities.

When Molly finished her meal, which she thoroughly enjoyed, she made sure to let Chef Willie know how it was.

"The catfish and taters were real good, Chef Willie! Someday, I'm gonna have you come cook for me at my place."

"I'd like that, but I don't think Porter would like it. You and he are still sweet on each other, ain't ya?"

Willie had known about Molly and Porter for a long time, and never said anything out of respect for their privacy except once.

He once told her, "Ain't healthy a black girl and a white boy being together, but it is what it is, and I'm happy for you!"

Willie had been a good friend of Molly and her family for years. It was almost as though he was an uncle. Hell, for all she knew, he may very well be.

Just then, Miss Mavis stepped out of the kitchen to say hello.

"Well, child, look at you. Did Willie feed you right? You need to come here more often." Miss Mavis had also known Molly a long time and treated her like a daughter.

"Good to see you, Miss Mavis. You're right; I need to come here more often. And yes, Chef Willie fed me good. Thanks for dinner, Chef Willie! Guess I'll be heading home now. Goodnight folks!"

"We'll see you Chief! You come on in anytime." They both replied as Molly left.

When she stepped out of the restaurant, Molly noticed Judy Waverly's car go past.

"Hmm, that looks like Judy Waverly's car. Wonder where she's going? Think when I see Porter tomorrow, I'm going to talk to him more about my suspicions."

As Molly was leaving Tom Parker was just arriving at the restaurant.

"Evening, Chief. Did we have the pleasure of feeding you tonight?"

"You sure did, and the catfish was fantastic. You've got the best chef in the South, and you'd better make sure you don't ever lose him!"

"Oh, I know that. Willie runs the place. I don't know what I'd do without him. I'll be sure and tell him you were pleased."

You'd damn sure better, Molly wanted to say but decided it was best not to for Chef Willie's sake.

"Thanks! Oh, I saw Mrs. Parker go by the bank earlier. She seemed annoyed that it was closed."

"Linda had some personal business to take care of, and I was off looking at the McClellan's place. Their online sales have given their business a big boost. They've decided to put an addition on to handle the extra business.

Who would have thought the Internet would make a little operation like theirs so successful? I'm considering their loan application."

Blocker's Bluff was fortunate to be close enough to several towns that had access to the Internet. Century Link was able to provide service to Blocker's Bluff via the telephone lines. At first, it was dial up but later they provided wireless service. It was a big convenience for the town's residents.

"Good for them. We could use a few more businesses here. Well, I got to go. You have a good night, Mayor!"

"You too, Chief!"

Molly got in her car and drove off. Her stomach was satisfied, but her curiosity wasn't. She just wanted to get home and curl up with the latest Jack Parson novel she was reading.

CHAPTER 13

Barbara was fuming when Tom came in the door, especially since there was no one at the bank when she went by earlier. For some reason, Linda Jacobs had left early, and she wondered why since Tom wasn't there. She began to wonder if he was having an affair with her and decided to confront him.

"Where the hell have you been? I went passed the bank earlier, and it was closed. You're up to something Tom, and I want to know what it is!"

Here we go again, he thought to himself. Barbara never lets up, and he was getting tired of her insinuations and her incessant questioning.

"Get a grip on yourself, Barbara, for God's sake. I spent the afternoon at the McClellan's place looking at their plans for expansion since I'm considering a loan for them. After that, I had dinner at the restaurant. If you don't believe me, ask Ed McClellan and Molly."

He was challenging her, but she still didn't believe him and made it obvious.

"I just might do that! Why was the bank closed so early?"

"You can't be serious, Barbara. Look nothing is going on. Can't you give it a rest? The bank closed because Linda had some personal business to take care of."

"Was it with you?"

He was tired of her accusations and seriously considered spending the night at the bank, but it wouldn't look good to folks if he did. He'd make a threat to see her reaction.

"I've had it! I can't stay here. I'm going to spend the night at the bank. Maybe tomorrow you'll come to your senses and realize that this is getting way out of hand."

"You do that, and don't come back!"

She caught him off guard as he never expected her to kick him out of the house.

"Are you serious? What's happening to you, Barbara? You never used to be like this. Is it because of my trips to Atlanta? I told you I have business there, and I can't discuss it with you. Just not yet."

She slapped her hand on the nearby table. "When Tom? When will you discuss it with your wife? You've never been this secretive, and always shared things with me. What's changed?"

No matter how much she pried and nagged, he wasn't about to tell her. He didn't trust her to keep his secret.

"I just can't, Barbara. I've got too much going on, and I don't want to spoil things prematurely. I trust you, but this is something I can't discuss with you, at least not yet. Just give me more time and space!"

She decided to relent one more time, but her patience was wearing thin. Maybe she should let him sleep at the bank. It would teach him a lesson, and he'd know that she meant business.

"Okay, Tom, this one time, but I won't wait forever. Sooner or later you'll have to tell me, or I'll find out for myself."

She was still pressing him and hoping to make him give in and tell her.

"What does that mean?"

She realized he was worried now, but it was best if she didn't make him sleep at the bank. It wouldn't look good for either one of them.

"You'll see, but if I have to wait, then you need to know that I mean what I say." The lines on her forehead furrowed. "You don't have to spend the night at the bank. You can stay here. You'd have to explain if anyone knew you weren't sleeping in your home, but tonight you have to sleep in one of the kid's rooms."

She made a trade-off to see how he liked sleeping by himself. It wouldn't be any different for her. Sleeping with him was like sleeping alone.

"Fine! I can handle that. Goodnight then!"

"Same to you and enjoy yourself, Tom!"

His mouth pursed unappreciative of her comment but chose to ignore it. Parker had other things on his mind, and although displeased, at least he wouldn't have to spend the night at the bank and explain it in the morning.

He turned, walked away and almost said out loud, "Damn her, what the hell does she mean she'll find out herself? She's going to ruin everything."

At least things in Atlanta were safe from her for now, but he wasn't sure about Linda and him. He'd have to tell Linda that they needed to cool it down for a while—which meant he had to tell her about Barbara.

It also meant that he might be forced to confide in Linda sooner than planned. Melanie wasn't going to like this new development, but he had no choice. He couldn't let Barbara spoil his big chance. The project had to happen. It meant a great deal for him and the town.

Sleeping alone in the kid's room wouldn't be so bad since sleeping with Barbara was practically like sleeping alone.

CHAPTER 14

Two months later, Molly was on her way to Porter's Island when she noticed that same fancy boat going around the island. She slowed down, retrieved her binoculars, and checked it out.

There didn't seem to be anyone on board at first, but then she noticed a woman dressed in a bikini looking back at her with binoculars. The woman must have noticed her because she started waving. Molly waved back and continued to Porter's Island.

She thought the incident was strange and wondered if the woman was just curious or if it was something else? Porter has to hear about this.

When Molly got to the dock, she was surprised to see Porter waiting for her. It was odd since he'd never met her at the dock. She usually had to yell for him.

"Mornin, Molly! Happy to see you!"

"What's with the greeting? You sick or something? You never meet me here."

The corners of his mouth hiked up. "Just being hospitable. Can't a man greet his best lady like a normal person?"

"You're not normal, Porter. You want something, don't you?"

"Aw, come on Molly, be a good girl. Here let me help you!"

There was a first time for everything but being polite wasn't something Porter would do. Cantankerous, yes, but nice, hell no! Something must be wrong.

"Who the hell are you? What happened to John Porter?"

"Molly, be civil now, or I won't invite you to spend the night."

"Who said I was spending the night?"

"If I beg, will you?"

Now this was more like him, but he would never beg for anything. He wanted something, Molly extended her arm toward him.

"Just give me a hand, you damn fool!"

"Hell, Molly, you didn't even notice the repairs I made to the dock. Harlan Thomas also complained about it, so I told him to bring me some lumber and pylons the next time he delivered my fuel. He brought a case of beer, which I paid for, and he stayed and helped me."

Molly's eyelids hoisted. "Now, that's something! I should have noticed it when I got here. Looks good, Porter and much safer too."

They unloaded her boat and brought everything into the cabin. Old George greeted Molly as he always did with a paw shake. She gave him a big treat, and kissed him.

When Molly entered the cabin, she couldn't believe what she saw. All the clutter was gone, as Porter had put things away. She reached for her gun and removed it from her holster.

"Put your hands up! Who the hell are you? What did you do with John Porter?"

"Take it easy Molly, and put that damn thing away before you shoot one of us!"

"Ain't no bullets in it anyway. Got, no need for them and you know that. Guess you are John Porter after all. What did you do?"

"I cleaned things up. You've been nagging about it, so I did what you wanted. Pretty good job, huh? Think I could get a job as an interior designer?"

"You wish! Excellent job Porter. I'm proud of you!"

"Does that mean I get laid tonight?"

"Damn, you just don't give up, do you?"

"Not when it comes to sex with you."

Old George walked over to Molly, extended a paw, and then kissed her when she bent down. He knew she had her hands full and was offering his commiseration.

"Now Old George knows how to treat a lady. Thanks, Old George. I love you!"

Old George wandered off, circled his blanket and dropped down.

"How about me? You love me too, don't you?"

"Sometimes, I think all you love is yourself. Of course, I love you. Who else besides Old George could love an old fool like you? Now you want me to fix us lunch, or can you do it?"

How about that? She said she loved him. Molly was weakening, and if she wasn't careful, she might fall for one of his proposals.

"I already got it fixed. Peanut butter and jelly sandwiches!"

Molly shook her head and lowered the corners of her mouth.

"I should have known better than to ask. Put those provisions over here. I bought you something special. I had Chef Willie fix us sandwiches. You got ham on rye, I got ham and cheese, and Old George gets a steak bone."

When Old George heard steak bone, he almost knocked the two of them over with excitement. Molly gave him his bone, and he wandered off with it.

"Damn! You sure you don't want to marry me, Molly?"

"What and be your babysitter for life? Never gonna happen. We're good the way we are. Let's not spoil it."

"I'm never gonna stop trying. You know I love you, always have, and always will!"

"Same here, old man!"

That was probably the first time they've ever admitted their true feelings to each other and twice now. Hell just might freeze over if this keeps up.

After lunch, Molly told him about the incident with the boat. She also mentioned the Parkers.

"So what do you think, Porter? Doesn't it strike you as suspicious?"

"You mean the boat or the Parkers?"

"Both. You damn fool! Don't you ever listen?"

"Well as for the boat." He paused and narrowed his eyes. "Wait! Why you calling me a damn fool? You want my opinion or not?"

Molly made a first for her. "I'm sorry, you're not an old fool." It was an apology, but she still considered him an old fool.

"That's better. I'm thinking we may have to ride out that way and see what's happening. It could be just city folk partying or some folk from Paris Island having some fun. We could just go out a ways and take a look the next time you come."

"And the Parkers?"

"That may need some thinking. Could be the Parkers are having some problems or could be nothing. Is he still making trips to Atlanta?"

"About every month and I have a suspicion something else is going on, but I can't put my finger on it."

"When you got more, you let me know. You always were able to figure things out. Let's hope it's nothing illegal.

"I'd sure like to follow him to Atlanta and see what he's up to."

"Maybe we could do that one day, but for now, let's hold off. What say we go fishing?"

They went fishing and had a very successful outing. Later Porter fried their catch. After dinner the three of them sat on the porch and watched the sun go down.

He reached for Molly's hand and led her to his bed where he took her breath away as he made love to her.

Porter did love Molly and wished she would say yes to his proposals. He knew he was a fool years ago when he let her get away and has regretted it every day.

He thought maybe Molly was right. What they had was close to marriage except she lived on the mainland, and he sheltered himself on the island.

In the morning, Porter took Old George out to do his business. He was looking offshore and noticed the boat Molly mentioned. It was going the opposite way from yesterday. He became curious.

When he and Old George returned, Molly had coffee and breakfast waiting. Damn, if this wasn't what a wife did for her husband, he told himself.

He walked over and kissed Molly. "You know when you do things like this I think you're my bride."

"Shut up and eat your breakfast. You damn old fool!"

He ignored her remark. "Saw that boat you mentioned yesterday. It was going the other way. Wonder what they were doing out all night?"

"Been trying to tell you something wasn't right."

"I'm starting to believe you. Next time you come, we'll take a look-see."

After breakfast, Molly gathered her things, said good-bye to Old George, and walked to the dock with Porter by her side. He took her in his arms and said he would miss her.

"You know I love you, don't you, Molly?"

"I know, and I love you too. Now I got to go. See you next time!"

That was the third time in two days they said they loved each other. Maybe Molly was weakening, or maybe it was because they had sex the night before. She pushed off, and as she left the dock, he stood there watching her fade away.

When she was completely out of sight, he got Old George and took him for a walk.

"I sure miss her as soon as she leaves, Old George."

Old George barked. He missed her too.

CHAPTER 15

Melanie was proud of what she had accomplished. The operation was named Strategic Investments, a limited partnership. She rented an office and had it furnished to look like a small investment firm. It wasn't lavish. She wanted potential marks to feel like they were dealing with a respectable firm. She even hired an administrative assistant and had her brother clean up and wear a suit.

Johnny looked like an investment officer, but he would spend most of his time out of the office. Melanie even had business cards made up for him. So far, Johnny was doing a good job with his role. She was certain even Parker would be pleased.

She was able to secure a few would-be investors and felt it wouldn't be long before she had their money. They wanted to meet Parker and be certain there was a bonafide title to the property and a survey.

Parker said he had an old survey but would get an updated one. He also had the title but was not going to transfer ownership until the partnership was secured.

The title would be transferred to the partnership after one million in limited partnerships was sold. Parker would be the general partner with management control. The investors would remain as limited partners with no control over partnership activities.

Melanie was having the partnership agreement prepared by an attorney for Parker's approval. When he arrived in Atlanta, she hoped to have everything in place for his approval. She wanted him to pony up more money so prospective marks would see that they had some financial assets.

Parker arrived at three in the afternoon, and when he saw the office, he was pleased. He was greeted by the administrative assistant and noticed how professional she was. She escorted him to Melanie's office and asked if she could get him anything.

"Yes please, a Coke would be fine."

The assistant escorted him to Melanie's office and went to get his Coke.

"Tom, it's good to see you. How was the drive?" She feigned that cute smile of hers.

"It was okay. Thanks for asking. The place looks nice, Melanie. Very professional looking and I like the administrative assistant. She seems pleasant and capable. You did well."

"Glad you approve, and you'll be even happier when you see Johnny. He looks like a real investment officer. I didn't have enough money to hire a real one, but he's just window dressing until we can hire someone." She was good at making up stories.

"As long you can keep him controlled. It's not as though he'll be seeing prospects." Parker closed the door for privacy. "Speaking of prospects, do we have any yet?"

"I've got three potential investors, but they want to see a current survey and the title to the property. You have them, don't you?"

"Yes, but the title is staying in my name until I'm comfortable transferring it to the partnership. I'm firm on that!"

"That's okay." It wasn't okay, but Melanie had to go along if she wanted more money. "Once they know you're the GP, they'll accept that.

Just then the door opened, and her assistant stepped in.

"Stephanie, this is Tom Parker. He's the general partner in a project we're putting together and very crucial to us. You'll be seeing quite a bit of him. Treat him nice."

"Nice to meet you, Mr. Parker! Here's your Coke."

When she bent over to give him his Coke, Parker couldn't help notice her assets. It helped that she was wearing a low-cut top that offered a fantastic view.

She leaned forward to shake his hand and give him another look.

"Thank you, Stephanie. It's a pleasure meeting you."

"You too, Mr. Parker."

Stephanie left, and Melanie got up and closed the door. Tom stood and took her in his arms.

"Not now, Tom and not here. Wait until later in your hotel room. We have business to take care of!"

"Okay." He was disappointed, but the expectation of later satisfied him. "Hey, that Stephanie sure is a looker. Where'd you find her?"

Melanie was annoyed with his comment. She felt he was an idiot, and his obsession with women could cause her trouble.

"Don't get any ideas, Tom. I got her from a temp agency. She worked here for a few weeks when we were getting the office set up. I asked her if she would be interested in a full-time position. She liked that we were a startup and agreed to come on board. She has excellent credentials."

What Melanie didn't know was that her real name wasn't Stephanie. No one knew who she was. She was from a small town in Georgia and moved to Atlanta after a divorce to start a new life and career. Her first job was with a temp agency at a construction site. She enjoyed the freedom that temp jobs offered, so she continued doing it. Eventually, she wound up working for Melanie.

"So, Melanie, what do I have to do to get these potential investors on board?"

"To begin with, you're going to have to come up with more money. We can't continue on an empty bank account. I told you we initially needed 50K, and all you've given me is fifteen. You have to come up with the money, and it has to be very soon!" She was pressing him and good at it.

Her request for very soon rattled him "Okay! I'll take care of it when I get back to Blocker's Bluff. Speaking of that, I have two things to tell you. Both could become problems. One I can resolve, but the other is touchy."

Melanie was suddenly worried. "What's the problem? Not your wife, I hope?"

"Yeah, she keeps nagging me about my trips here and now is threatening to find out what's going on. So far she thinks I'm having an affair. She's right about that, but she also thinks there's more. I don't want to let her in on what's going on. She would freak and spoil everything." He nervously rubbed his chest. "What do you think I should do?"

Melanie didn't want to hear this. She didn't need a meddling wife screwing up her plans.

"Hold off telling her anything for a while longer. Let her believe you're having an affair, which you are. We can deal with her later."

"But I think she's threatening to follow me."

"If she does, we'll handle it then. What's the other thing?"

His expression suddenly reflected concern. "I'm not sure what you mean by, handle it, and I don't think I want to know!"

"You don't," she replied.

His eyes narrowed from worry, and he continued. "The other thing is my bank manager. She's asking questions, and sooner or later I'll have to tell her what I'm doing. I'm taking money from the bank, and she's going to find out. I won't be able to hide it from her."

Melanie didn't want anyone else involved in the scam. It's what had caused things to go wrong in the past but, if necessary, she would overlook it this time.

"If you have to let her in on this, then do so, but be careful how you do it. Can she be trusted?"

"I think so. We have somewhat of a secret of our own."

He didn't want Melanie to know about Linda, but his comment slipped out before he realized what he said.

"Are you banging her?" Melanie was never one to mince words. "What a schmuck you are!"

She was worried he was going to spoil her plans because he couldn't keep his pants zipped. If he did, she swore he'd pay dearly. She'd have Johnny take care of him.

"Look, what I do away from Atlanta is none of your business!"

"It is if it affects this project. Now let's go see the lawyer and get those papers signed."

"And afterward?"

"We'll see. After what you've told me, I'm not sure what to do about you."

She was beginning to realize she'd made a big mistake sleeping with Parker. The basic rules of a con were you don't let the mark get too close to you, and you don't get too personal with the target. She violated both rules.

At the lawyer's office, Parker executed the documents forming the limited partnership without a transfer of title.

The agreement included a clause that once fifty percent of the limited partnerships were sold, with a minimum of one million in capital raised, transfer would occur. The lawyer validated Tom's survey for the agreement.

When they were done, Melanie agreed to meet Parker in his hotel room. She was violating the rules again and hoped it didn't come back to haunt her. She had to wean herself away from sleeping with him.

CHAPTER 16

The nearly six-hour drive from Atlanta to Blocker's Bluff on Interstate 26 gave Tom ample time to consider everything that was happening and some thought as to what he was going to do next.

He had a lot to think about Melanie's comment concerning handling Barbara—which made him nervous. He still wasn't sure what she meant and hoped she didn't mean causing harm to her. Tom couldn't live with himself if that were to happen. But how could he keep Barbara at bay?

Linda was a different situation. He could handle her. Their affair and her feelings for him should be enough to bring her on board. Somehow he had to find a way to convince her. Maybe after they did their thing in his office, he'd make an attempt.

However he did, it would have to be soon. Linda would surely notice he had taken $50,000 out of bank funds. If the Bank Examiners were to show up suddenly, he'd need her help to hide it from them. She was very smart and surely could find a way to help him.

He had to formulate a plan as soon as he arrived home as time was of the essence. $15,000 was one thing, but another fifty was a bigger problem. He'd worry about Barbara after he dealt with Linda.

When Tom was close to town, he called Linda on his cell phone. He wasn't going to give her any details but wanted to get the ball rolling.

"Hello, Tom, is that you? Where are you?"

"I'm on my way home from Atlanta, and I need to talk to you. I want to run something by you. But not over the phone, it's too private and has to do with my trips to Atlanta."

"Okay. When do you want to get together, or do you want to wait until Monday at the bank?

"I haven't decided yet, but I wanted to give you a heads up. Better yet, let's wait until Monday morning when we see each other. You're still planning on getting in early, aren't you?

"Yes, Tom, same as every Monday. I'll see you then. You take care and drive safely."

"Thanks, Linda."

Maybe it wouldn't be so difficult getting Linda's help, after all, he decided.

CHAPTER 17

Just as she had every Monday morning, Linda was at the bank waiting for Parker to arrive. As soon as Parker arrived, Linda greeted him, and then followed him to his office. She closed the door and Parker, as usual, sat in his chair behind his desk, and they went about their regular ritual.

Linda straightened her skirt and asked. "So Tom, what do you want to discuss with me?"

At first, she thought it might have something to do with their relationship or her job. The way he acted so far didn't seem like it was about either. She was curious to know what he had in mind.

Parker scratched his chin. "Linda, I have something vital to discuss with you. It has to be in strictest confidence, and you might not like what it's about, but I need your help and your support. It's very crucial."

Her eyebrows lowered. "Tom, you know you can trust me with anything and whatever it is, it's absolutely between the two of us." She elevated the corners of her mouth. "Isn't everything we do that way? You don't have to worry. Nothing would stop me from supporting you. It's not illegal or about the bank, is it?"

He was surprised by the question. Linda was too smart, but she said she would support him, and whatever it was she would keep it in strict confidence. But illegal and about the bank might be a different matter.

She waited for a reply, but he was silent.

"Tom, what is it? You're not answering my question. It does have something to do with the bank, and it may not be legal, doesn't it?" Her voice became gruff. "Tell me and what does it have to do with Atlanta?"

He hesitated and then decided to tell her. If he didn't, she wouldn't help him.

"Linda, the trips to Atlanta are about a real estate project I'm trying to put together. It involves the land I own west of town. Someone in Atlanta is working with me on it."

There was suddenly enthusiasm in his speech.

"So far we've put together a limited partnership with me as the general partner. We're working on securing investors as limited partners. It has to remain confidential until we have enough investors to get the project off the ground. I promise if I succeed, it will be good for the town and everyone.

"The problem is I have to supply the seed money and the initial cash flow to get things started. So far I have invested $15,000, but I need another fifty."

What he initially did was use cash from the vault as deposits to his account and then purchased a bank draft for the money payable to the partnership. He handled the tickets himself and had the tellers run them through their work. They didn't ask any questions since he had the authority, but $50,000 was a different situation.

Linda's eyes narrowed with concern. "Tom, you don't have that much cash on hand. Where are you going to get it?" She clasped her hands to her cheeks. "Oh, no, don't tell me you plan on using bank funds? That's illegal, and you could get in serious trouble and possibly even end up going to prison."

"I know! That's why I need your help and your support."

"You want to make me complicit in your scheme?" She envisioned an orange jumpsuit in her future. "I don't want to go to prison. I'd do anything for you. You know that, but prison is different, Tom!"

"Linda, I've already used bank funds, but I need the extra fifty. I knew you would eventually find out about the money and would question me, but I need your help. I won't let anything happen to you. I promise!"

"Tom, you're asking an awful lot. I have to think about this. When do you want an answer?"

"I need an answer by the end of the week; otherwise, I have no choice but to just do it. You could always say you weren't aware of any impropriety."

"You know that wouldn't fly with the Bank Examiners or the authorities. If I don't report it, that make me complicit." She took a step back. "You're not leaving me with much of a choice. By telling me, I'm already guilty. I'll let you know, but this is wrong, Tom, and appalling!"

"I know. I'm sorry Linda, but I trust you. Not even Barbara knows, and I'm not going to tell her. She's making threats, but that's because she thinks I'm having an affair in Atlanta."

"Are you, Tom?"

He didn't answer. How could he? If he said yes, Linda might turn on him. If he lied, she would see right through him. He couldn't win whichever way he chose, so he didn't say anything.

"You son of a bitch" She clenched her fists. "Is she getting your jollies off too? And what does that make me? Your whore! How could you do this to me? I've given you years of loyalty. The way I feel right now is that I should report you to the banking authorities and save my ass. I don't know what I'm going to do. I'm taking the day off. Goodbye!" She stormed out of the bank and left him to ponder her words.

CHAPTER 18

Old George was outside napping when suddenly his ears perked. He stood up, looked to the sky, and barked. Porter was sitting on the porch relaxing in his rickety old rocker. He'd had the rocker for almost twenty years and sure could use a new one.

He noticed Old George's anxiety. "What's up, Old George, is it Molly you sense?"

Of course, he couldn't answer, but Porter had learned over the years that he could tell what Old George was saying by his body language and his bark. His loud rapid bark without a wagging tail usually meant danger. If he barked and wagged his tail, it signified Molly was coming, or he wanted dinner.

For the past six months, Old George had been acting strange, and Porter still hadn't figured out what was bothering him. Usually, he could understand what Old George was excited about, but this one had him baffled. There was no sign of Molly, so it wasn't about her, and he couldn't see anything off in the distance. Something had the dog spooked. He'd ask Molly what she thought the next time she visited.

"Old George, I know something's bothering you, but for the life of me I can't figure it out. Sometimes, I wish you could talk like a human. It sure would make life easier for the two of us."

If Old George could speak, he'd certainly say, "Then I would have to put up with your insane antics like Molly does! No thanks!"

Old George took the pointer position, barked twice, and was about to bolt before he finally settled on the floor. Something at sea sure was bothering him.

CHAPTER 19

In the bank parking lot, Barbara had been sitting in her car ever since she followed Parker that morning. She thought she'd parked where her car would be inconspicuous, but when Linda came out of the bank, she gave a quick glance in Barbara's direction.

Barbara would have ducked down, but she was sure Linda saw her, and why hide? She'd made her decision to start following Parker around town. If Linda saw her, so be it. The bank was the first place she chose to spy on him because she was curious as to why some days he went in so early when it was Linda's job to open the bank.

"Wonder what's up with Linda? She doesn't look too happy, and why is she leaving so early?" Barbara asked herself. "The bank hasn't even opened yet."

She sat and waited to see if Parker would also leave the bank. If something was happening between them, she'd know when she followed him, but he didn't leave and stayed until closing time. The only people that entered were the tellers and local customers, and Barbara knew them all.

Barbara decided today was a waste of time, but at least she was doing something. Judy had told her not to, but she couldn't let it fester any longer. Eventually, he would make a mistake. For now, she'd best get home before he did.

Barbara pulled out of the parking lot just as Molly drove by on her way to her office. They waved at each other and drove on.

Molly thought it strange that Barbara Parker was just coming from the bank. Tom Parker's car was still in the bank parking lot. She was curious as to why Barbara was making so many trips into town and always going by the bank.

CHAPTER 20

Tonight Molly was spending the night at the station and would sleep in the jail cell. She'd make rounds later and be on call. Nothing usually happened to be of concern, but it was her responsibility. At least, she had her book to read.

Molly was just heading out to make rounds when she noticed Judy Waverly's car leaving town. Judy must have a client that wants to discuss buying or selling some real estate, she thought. It wasn't that unusual for Judy to make evening visits.

Everything was quiet and around midnight she decided to catch some shut-eye. In the morning, Molly was up and heading to Parker's restaurant for an early breakfast. She noticed Tom Parker pulling into the bank parking lot. She thought it strange that two mornings in a row he'd arrived early.

Usually, Linda Jacobs was already there when he arrived, but this morning her car wasn't in the lot. Parker looked around for her car. Seeing it wasn't there, he went into the bank.

Just as Molly was entering the restaurant, she noticed Barbara's car pass.

"Wonder what that's all about?" Molly asked herself and went on in for breakfast.

"Morning, Chief! You're up early."

"Morning, Chef Willie! I just finished my all-nighter."

"Why you keep calling me Chef Willie? Can't you just call me Willie? I've known you so long that we're almost family."

"Sorry! Just being respectful. You've earned the title, and I'm not going to change what I call you. You're right; we are almost family and for all, I know we could be, but you'll always be Chef Willie to me."

"Have it your way. I'll just keep calling you Chief then."

"Okay by me. How are the grits this morning?"

"Same as always. You just don't come in and have em as often. Sit down I'll fix you a plate with some eggs, bacon, and biscuits."

"You're gonna fatten me up, Chef Willie!"

"Somebody's got to look after you."

"Now you sound like my dad."

"He was a good man and Mrs. Dickson was a wise lady. You come from good stock!"

"Don't I know it? Now how about that breakfast?"

"Coming up!"

"Say, what's Miss Mavis doing this morning?"

"She's busy baking and getting the bakery and general store ready for opening. I'll tell her you were by."

"Thanks, I appreciate that."

Chef Willie fixed Molly a hearty plate and a strong cup of coffee. She ate everything as she was usually hungry in the mornings and liked a good breakfast—ever since she was a kid.

"Say, I noticed the Mayor arrived at the bank early this morning, and Linda wasn't there yet. I also saw Mrs. Parker's car. Is that usual?"

"Well, Mrs. Parker driving by early is unusual, but Mr. Parker getting to the bank isn't. He does it a few times a week, but usually, Miss Jacobs is there before him. Strange, you say she wasn't there yet?"

"No, she wasn't. You know Chef Willie; I'm beginning to think some strange things are going on at that bank."

"You want me to keep a lookout?"

Chef Willie was the best person to watch the bank since he had a view of it from the restaurant. However, he had enough with running the restaurant, and Molly sure didn't want to add to his burden or get him in trouble with Parker.

"I'm just curious, but if you do notice anything let me know and keep it between us. Just don't go out of your way, you're busy enough."

"Okay, Chief."

CHAPTER 21

Linda Jacobs lived in a small bungalow east of town. Judy Waverly helped her pick it out, and Tom Parker provided the financing with a very liberal mortgage.

It was furnished to suit a single woman. Not too fancy and with some nice touches. Linda had a keen eye for decorating and kept things simple.

Outside, azalea bushes and day lilies adorned the front yard, especially along the walk leading to the front door. Linda did all the gardening herself including mowing what little lawn she had.

She was expecting company just like every Monday evening and had prepared a light meal for the two of them. Linda needed to confide in someone. Parker had dropped a bombshell on her, and she couldn't deal with it by herself.

The doorbell rang, and Linda let in her guest. They hugged each other then sat in the kitchen with a glass of wine. Linda and her companion were not heavy drinkers. An occasional glass of wine was all they shared.

Over dinner, Linda decided to unburden herself as she was upset and couldn't keep her secret any longer.

"That son of a bitch!" she yelled. "Parker went too far this time!"

"What happened? Are you going to tell me about it or keep it bottled up? Just tell me, please!"

Linda wasn't sure what kind of reaction she'd get once she revealed the day's events. But she needed a respite.

"I told you, he's been making trips to Atlanta. Well, he finally said why. It seems he has a deal in the works with someone there. It has to do with developing the land he owns west of town. He and his partner have formed a limited partnership to raise funds by selling individual partnerships. Parker's the general partner. Oh, he also has a piece up there."

"You mean like in a piece of ass?"

"Yes, well fuck him!" Linda threw her fork at the wall and watched it bounce to the floor.

"Oh, you are pissed."

"You bet I am, but that's not the worst of it. Parker's using bank funds to start his supposed deal. Now, he wants to use even more, and he wants me to look the other way. Can you believe that bastard?"

"Yes, but, Linda that's illegal."

"No kidding. Who the hell does he think he is?"

"How much this time?"

Linda didn't want to say but answered to avoid more questions.

"So far $15,000 but now he intends to use another fifty. He wants my help hiding the fact that he's embezzling bank funds. Just by telling me and me not doing anything makes me complicit."

Linda hadn't by realized that by revealing the information, she might be making someone else complicit.

"What are you going to do?"

"I don't know. I lose either way. If the Bank Examiners find out about it, they could trace things way back, and I would be in bigger trouble."

"What are you talking about way back? Have you been doing the same thing?"

Linda realized she was about to reveal more damaging information.

She took a sip of wine and leaned back. "How do you think I was able to pay for all those vacations we took?"

"Linda, you could go to jail, maybe even prison!"

"I know, that's why I'm in a dilemma."

"Sounds like you don't have much choice but to go along. If you turn Parker in, it will spark an investigation, and they might find about what you've done."

It's what Linda was afraid of, and all she could think of was to protect the two of them. Parker had put her in a real bind.

"That's what has me so mad." She slapped her hand on the kitchen counter. "Screw him and I screw myself. He wants a decision on Friday."

"He's not giving you much time, is he?"

"No, and to make matters worse, Barbara's been giving him a hard time about his trips. She suspects he's having an affair. As long as she suspects it's in Atlanta, that's one less worry for me. As far as Tom Parker and me, it's finished! Let him find someone else or let his Atlanta whore take care of his needs."

It sounded good in principle, but Linda knew that was not the answer.

"Good for you. I have one question, though. By telling me about this, does it make me complicit?"

Linda now had a bigger problem and finally realized the damage she'd done to their friendship. She envisioned handcuffs around her companion's wrists.

"Oh shit! I didn't think about that. Yes, it does, but I'll make sure you're never involved. As long as we keep it our secret you're safe. I swear I'll go to my grave protecting you!"

Linda meant every word she said as long as they kept the secret between them her companion was safe.

"I love you, Linda!"

"Same here. I wish you could spend the night."

Linda knew it was impossible especially now, with the way things were.

"Me too, but you have neighbors. And although they're not close by, it wouldn't look good me leaving in the morning. We do have the rest of the night, though. Let's make the best of it."

It's all they had and always made good use of their time together.

"The best thing about me moving back to Blocker's Bluff was reconnecting with you. We were good together before you wanted marriage. You tried to be something you weren't."

"Yes, but now we're together again. Come on; I want to make love to you!"

"I've been waiting for you to say that, it's what I need right now!"

They went to Linda's bedroom, undressed and ruffled the sheets.

CHAPTER 22

When Molly pulled up to the dock, Porter was waiting. She thought it unusual and wondered if something was wrong. It wasn't Old George because he was by Porter's side.

"What's the matter? You don't usually meet me here."

He waved his hand at her. "Come on let's unload. I want to run something by you, and maybe we might go for a boat ride."

"Sure, but you have me concerned. At first, I thought something might be wrong with Old George, but I see he's at your side."

"It concerns Old George, but let's put these things inside."

Together they brought the provisions into the cabin. When everything was in its proper place, Molly asked him what was wrong.

"For the past several weeks, Molly, Old George has been acting strangely at times. He gets up stares out to sea, growls and seems agitated. I haven't noticed anything out there, but he's like that for about twenty to thirty minutes then calms down."

"What do you think it is?" she asked.

"Don't know, but I'm wondering if it has anything to do with that boat you keep seeing?"

"You want to take a boat ride and see if there's anything out there?"

"Yes! You up for it?"

"What about Old George? Do we leave him here?"

"If we take my boat, he can come with us. Mine's bigger 'n yours."

"You want lunch first, or do we go now?"

"Let's go now."

They headed to the dock and his boat. Molly's was ten feet long, but his was fifteen with a small cabin. It also had two outboards and was much faster in the water, especially in rough seas.

They left the dock and Porter steered straight for the deep water. When they were several miles from the island, he turned to the leeward side and made for the outer bank.

Fifteen miles out, Porter throttled down and searched the shoreline and the skies. Old George was calm, so Porter figured there was nothing to see. He went out to about twenty-five miles from the island and still saw nothing so headed back towards the isle.

Hidden in the marshes far enough away to be unseen by Porter and Molly was the boat Molly often saw go by the island. On board, a man and a woman were watching with binoculars.

The man said to the woman, "Doesn't look like they see anything. We may have to watch them and be more careful."

"That's not the same boat I see when we pass by the island. There's usually just the woman. I wonder who the guy is, and it looks like there's a dog with them?"

"Maybe he's the one living on the island?"

"It looks like they're leaving."

"Good, we'll wait thirty minutes then make our pickup and go on north."

Porter decided to head back toward his place. They hadn't noticed anything out of the ordinary, but Old George seemed a little restless only not like the other times. Maybe it had to do with the weather?

"What do you think, Porter?"

"Don't know, but something's making Old George nervous."

"I noticed that, plus I got this feeling like someone was watching us."

"I did too, but I didn't see anything on the shoreline. We are way out, though. Let's go home and have lunch."

He pulled up to the dock; hitched the boat, and they headed to the cabin. They had lunch, went for a walk, and afterward sat on the dock and did some fishing for dinner. With what they caught, they had their dinner for the evening. Molly was glad because she didn't want to fix a meal.

Porter and Molly spent the night in his rickety old bed. As usual, it was uncomfortable, but he made it worthwhile. He always did.

In the morning, she fixed breakfast and said she had to get back to town. She wished she could stay longer, but she was the Chief of Police and had responsibilities, unlike him.

As she was leaving, Molly still had that weird feeling of being watched yesterday.

"I can't shake that feeling from yesterday. What say we go out again next time I come?"

"If it will make you feel better, we can. You take care on your way back to town, Molly."

"Thanks. You know, sometimes you're not such a mean old bastard."

"Keep talking dirty and I won't let you off the island."

They laughed as he pushed her boat away from the dock and left for town.

Old George wagged his tail as she pulled away.

The two of them decided to take a walk as both were feeling disappointed that Molly left.

Porter may enjoy his isolation on the island, but he loved when Molly visited.

So did Old George.

CHAPTER 23

Seven-thirty Friday morning Linda arrived at the bank and right behind her was Parker. Before they entered the bank, he asked Linda if she'd made a decision yet.

"And good morning to you too!" she snapped. "Yes, I have, but wait until we're in the bank."

"Okay."

Neither of them noticed Barbara's car go by at that same moment. Barber didn't want it to be obvious she was following Tom. She thought it was strange that all week, Linda had been arriving at 8:30 except on Monday and today.

Once inside the bank, Parker went immediately to his office, sat behind his desk, and asked if Linda was going to join him?

"No, never again," she bristled. "Those days are over. You've got your whore in Atlanta, let her satisfy you because I never will again!"

He hoisted his palms. "Okay, I understand. You're still angry about Monday. We'll let things cool down and get back to normal."

"You stupid son of a bitch!" she hollered. "There's no more normal. Get it through your head. I'm finished and over you!" She pointed at his groin. "You can keep your pants zipped up from now on!"

"Okay, Linda!" he yelled. "I get it but what about the other thing? What's your decision?"

"Just like that>" she replied and shook her head. "It's easy for you, isn't it, Tom? I'll do it, but I'll decide how we go about it. You're too damn stupid to do anything right!"

"Was that necessary?"

"Yes, it was."

"Okay already, what's your plan?"

"We'll create a fake mortgage borrower for sixty thousand dollars. That way it will look like there's nothing suspicious." He listened close as she continued. "We'll need to do the proper paperwork, and make monthly repayment, so it looks legitimate. That's going to be your problem, not mine."

"I like the idea." He narrowed his eyes. "If I didn't know better, I'd think you'd done this before."

Linda avoided his eyes and remained silent. She didn't want him to know that was how she managed to steal the funds from the bank, only she used installment loans mostly for autos. She repaid almost all but now thought it best to pay off the last two.

"You've got your plan, Tom, but you sign off on any mortgage. My name doesn't appear anywhere."

"No problem, I can do that, but I'll need your help with the paperwork."

"I'll take care of it."

Now that Tom had a plan to get the funds, he needed to let Melanie know. He also had to tell her about Linda just not right away.

"One more thing, Tom, I want to know your contact's name in Atlanta. If you don't tell me, then I'm not on board."

He straightened in his chair. "Do you really need to know?"

"Yes! Do you think I'm stupid? If I'm putting my career in jeopardy, and maybe my life, I want to know everything."

"Okay, but that's all for now. It has to be that way. Her name is Melanie Tifton."

Interesting, Linda thought. It's funny how her name pops up at strange times. What Parker didn't know was that Linda and Melanie crossed paths once before—a long time ago.

Outside, Barbara sat in her car waiting and watching. Since it was close to lunchtime, she decided to have lunch at the restaurant instead of driving home, so she's there in case Parker left the bank.

Parker and Jacobs worked most of the morning on the fake mortgage papers. It was Friday, and many of the townsfolk usually came in to do their banking.

Fortunately, most came in the afternoon, giving the two their privacy to work on the mortgage loan.

Linda decided to wait until Wednesday to complete the mortgage transaction. Doing it too soon would look suspicious. She backdated the application a few weeks, and had Parker's signature dated the previous Monday.

Everything was now in place for when the time came to initiate the plan. Linda locked the door and left. Parker went to the restaurant for dinner.

Barbara left, so she would be there when Tom came home after dinner.

CHAPTER 24

Since things had gone south after Parker's revelations, Linda needed a sounding board and someone she could trust. She had already shared some of what she and Parker were doing, and this Friday evening she'd reveal more. Nothing was said before or during dinner, but now that they were enjoying a glass of wine, the questions started.

"How did it go today?"

"It went well just as I planned it, "Linda replied.

"What did he say when you told him that you were through with his cheating dick?"

"He thought it was temporary until things quieted down, but I set him straight. You know what? I'm glad too. I wish I'd never got involved with him. How stupid I was?"

"You were just following your heart and sometimes that makes people blind to reality. Don't beat yourself up over Parker."

"You're right; that is what I'm doing. Thanks for the reality check." Linda's lips pursed. "I still have you, and that's all I need. What would I do without you?"

"And what would I do without you?"

"Let's forget about Parker and this whole mess. We've got most of the night to enjoy ourselves. I hope you can make me forget all this."

"I'll try! Are you sure you've covered all bases?"

"Yes! No more talk." Linda nodded toward the bedroom. "Let's use our time together, so that I can forget everything. I need a reprieve from this mess."

"No better time than now."

CHAPTER 25

Three months later, Linda went to Atlanta. She knew just where to go as she'd seen Melanie's card in Parker's office and made a note of the address. It was time to confront Melanie and let her know that she knew what was going on.

It wasn't the first time Melanie pulled a scam like the one she was doing with Parker, and that one almost cost Linda her job because she was naïve at the time. This time, she wasn't naive.

Linda entered the office, and Stephanie greeted her.

"May I help you?"

"I'd like to see Melanie, is she in?"

"Yes, but do you have an appointment?

"It's okay; I'll find my way. You don't need to trouble yourself."

"You can't just barge in!"

"I'm an old friend, so just relax!"

Linda went directly to Melanie's office and walked right in without knocking.

"Very impressive, Melanie, you've come a long way in the world. The administrative assistant is a new angle and a nice touch."

Melanie looked up and said. "Do I know you?"

"You sure do, it was a long time ago, so I'll refresh your memory. My name is Linda Jacobs, and I'm Tom Parker's bank manager."

Melanie's face turned white. She never expected to hear the name Linda Jacobs again and not in the same context as Tom Parker. She sensed trouble was coming.

"It certainly has been a long time. I'm surprised to see you. What brings you to Atlanta?"

"Oh, some real estate in Blocker's Bluff owned by Tom Parker. I'm sure you know what I'm talking about."

Stephanie stood in the doorway, started to say something, but Melanie waved her off.

"It's okay, Steph. She's an old friend of mine. Do me a favor, close the door and make sure I'm not disturbed."

"Sure, whatever!" She closed the door and went back to her desk. "I wonder what's going on in there. They may be old friends but Melanie sure didn't seem happy to see that woman and the mention of being Parker's bank manager. I'll listen in on their conversation." Stephanie pressed a button under the desk and picked up the phone.

"Sit down, Linda. What's on your mind?"

"I know what you and Parker are up to, but I'm sure he doesn't know what you're doing. Does he know about your past?"

"No, and I'd rather it stayed that way. According to Parker, you're part of this too so don't think about doing anything to jeopardize my plans. What is it you want?"

"Thanks to your pressuring Parker, he's made me an accomplice in his embezzlement scheme." Melanie's mouth formed a big O. "Surprise, now you know where he got the money from. How ironic! Melanie's caught up in something bigger than she expected."

"Parker never told me that's how he came about the funds. I swear Linda. I didn't know!"

"Then you're not as smart as I thought you were. Whatever scam you're working can't go on for long, and you may have to do something legitimate for once."

"What do you mean?"

"If things go wrong at the bank, the authorities are going to trace the funds to here, and it will be the Feds looking for you. We'll all go down. Parker's not going to cover your ass, and neither am I."

"I could pack up and quit now and fade away. You and Parker would be left to deal with the authorities."

"You could, but we'll work out a deal to help them find you and your whole world will come crashing down."

Melanie waved both hands. "Okay, let's not get ahead of ourselves. What do you propose?"

"Do you have any real investors?

"I have two who are ready to put up 50K each and another on the fence, but I can get him to commit."

"Yeah, I'm sure you can! I'm sure you're still using your body to get what you want, and that's how you hooked Parker. You haven't changed, Melanie."

"You don't have to get nasty."

"Like you didn't back then?" Linda wasn't about to make things easy with Melanie.

Melanie tilted her head and raised her palm. "I made a mistake. I'm sorry."

"Yeah sure, like I believe you! You get those investors to put up their money and find some more. Somehow this project has to get off the ground. You and Parker have left me no choice but to help, but you have to do something legitimate for once and stay with it."

"I've never done that before, but there's always a first time. Thanks, Linda. When this is over, I'll owe you."

Linda grinned. "And I'll be sure to collect. Oh, and one more thing. Parker's wife is following him around. It won't be long before she follows him here. She suspected me of having an affair with him but gave up on that idea."

"I thought you two were?"

"Not anymore. Not since he roped me into this. Now it's just you. You're going to regret getting involved with him. His weakness is his appetite for sex, which I'm sure you're well aware of, better be careful, Melanie."

"Thanks! I've been trying to push him away, but he's like a baby hungry for his momma's nipple. Honestly, I wish I hadn't gotten involved with him, but I'm in too deep."

"Like I said, be careful, Melanie. See you around."

Linda knew Melanie wouldn't heed her advice because Melanie never could make prudent decisions when they involved sex.

"You too. It was good seeing you again."

"Yeah, right!" Linda tersely replied.

Linda opened the door, said goodbye to Stephanie, and headed back to Blocker's Bluff. Melanie had much to think about, but Linda would have to watch her own back because Melanie could be extremely vindictive.

Unbeknownst to both of them, Stephanie had overheard their entire conversation.

CHAPTER 26

Twenty miles off the South Carolina coastline, a plane dipped low and came in for its drop. The pilot said, "Clear skies, open the door."

Once the plane was low enough, the co-pilot pushed three packages out the door, and the plane then started to climb. The pilot watched as they hit the water, radioed all clear, and took off to the south.

In a small cove hidden in the marshes, a boat watched as the plane made the drop and took off. Thirty minutes later, after receiving the all-clear sign from the pilot, the boat headed out to sea.

The woman on board checked the GPS and guided the man to the location. When they reached their destination, the woman used the hook to reach over the side and plucked a package from the water. She then did the same to the other two. When all three were on board, they headed north.

"Well, that went smoothly!" the man on board said.

"Yes, and it's a good thing we did it at night. Those two from the island might have been out, and then we'd have had trouble."

"If they keep snooping, we may have to do something about it."

"Don't be stupid." The woman replied. "That will only make trouble. We'll keep doing night drops until they stop snooping. Things are going as planned, let's not spoil it."

"You're right, but I don't like it."

"Too bad, get over it. After we make our drop, I'll make it up to you. You'll be a happy man!"

His eyes lit up, and he smiled. "Then let's get going because that bikini of yours is pushing my buttons. Aren't you cold?"

"No, I'm warm-blooded, but I'll put something over it to make you happy."

"That won't make me happy, but maybe you should."

"Sometimes, I wonder why I partnered up with you?"

"Because I've got the contacts and the boat, and you couldn't do this by yourself." He winked. "Besides, I'm good in bed!"

Her head shook. "Let's just get the hell out of here."

Unbeknownst to them, Porter and Old George were moored in the marshes a mile away and were watching. When Old George became agitated earlier, Porter decided to go out in his boat and have a look. He made sure he kept his running lights off so no one could see him coming.

It was a perfect night. The ocean was surprisingly calm, a crescent moon was in the sky, and there were plenty of stars. A good night for fishing in the event there was nothing to see, and as a precaution had his fishing gear on board.

When he first heard the plane he headed for shore where he had a clear view should anything occur. He waited and watched. When he saw the boat's running lights, he knew something was up.

"Wait until I tell Molly about this, Old George."

Old George wagged his tail. If he could speak, he'd tell Molly too.

When the boat took off north, Porter headed back to his dock.

"Old George, you got some kind a hearing, and you'd make a great detective. Good job! I would have missed that plane if it weren't for you. Let's go home."

If he could, Old George would have said, "That's why you bring me along. Without me, you're pretty much useless."

Porter pulled up to the dock, secured the boat, and then the two of them walked to the cabin. He got a beer for himself and a treat for Old George, and then sat on the porch to watch the stars in the sky.

"Sure is a pretty night, hey, boy?"

Old George wagged his tail and barked. He was proud of himself and Porter.

CHAPTER 27

After Linda had left, Melanie was shaken. She never in a million years thought she'd ever see her again. Linda was right; Melanie did almost cost Linda her job, and it almost cost Melanie much more. Now, she had a decision to make.

She thought about taking the $50,000 and getting out quick, but Parker said he could come up with more. If that were the case, she'd wait and then get out.

As Melanie sat contemplating the situation with a worried look on her face, Stephanie stood in the doorway.

Melanie looked up. "How long have you been standing there?

"Not long, but you look pretty worried. What was that all about?"

"Did you hear anything?"

"Some. How could I not? Your office isn't soundproof. I hear lots of things, Melanie!"

"What do you mean lots of things?"

"I'm not stupid. I know what's going on. You and Parker are working a scheme, and that Jacobs woman wants in on it. Am I correct?"

"You're smarter than I thought. Have you been spying on us, Steph?"

"Like I said, your office isn't soundproof. Want to tell me what's going on?"

"It's best you don't know."

"You should let me decide that. I'm a big girl, Melanie."

"I can see that, but I'm keeping you out of this. You'll thank me one day."

Melanie wasn't talking about Stephanie's height. It was one of the reasons she hired her. Men liked looking at a big girl especially one who filled out a top like Stephanie. Besides, Melanie also enjoyed observing.

"Maybe so, but it sounds like that Jacobs woman could make trouble for you, and I don't think I would like that."

"It's none of your business, Steph. Stay out of it for your own good!"

"I'll decide what's for my good."

Now Melanie not only had Linda Jacobs to worry about but Stephanie as well. She wasn't sure what Stephanie meant and was afraid it might mean trouble. Another damn issue, she told herself.

"I think we should close the office for today. Take the rest of the day off, Steph."

"Not much left of it anyway, but I could use the free time. Take care Melanie, if you can!" She closed the door and left.

Stephanie's comment was similar to Linda's, and it worried Melanie.

"Damn her; she's making me nervous. I've never had to deal with this many issues. I've got my brother to be concerned about, Parker and his pecker, and now these two damn women. I wonder what Bill McPayne would do?"

Melanie closed the office, went to her car, and drove home. What she didn't know was that Linda Jacobs followed her. However, Linda was unaware that Stephanie was right behind her.

When Stephanie left the office, she went to her car which was parked four spaces from Melanie's. She noticed Linda Jacobs had parked several rows away and was sitting in her car. Stephanie waited to see what Linda was planning.

When Melanie pulled out of the parking garage, Linda followed her, and Stephanie followed Linda.

"So that's what the bitch is up to," Stephanie said. "She's following Melanie to see where she lives."

Melanie led them both to her townhouse unaware that someone was following her. When she entered her townhouse, Linda drove on by and headed for Blocker's Bluff.

Once Stephanie was sure Linda was on her way to South Carolina, she decided that she needed to know where Jacobs lived and followed her.

It was a long drive for Linda, but she made it home before eleven, unaware of the car that had followed her all the way from Atlanta; the same car that went past her house as she was getting out of her vehicle.

Stephanie drove on by and said, "Gotcha bitch!" Then she drove on until she found a Motel 6 on Interstate 95 halfway between Blocker's Bluff and Atlanta. She'd drive the rest of the way in the morning.

Since she was there, Stephanie decided to make a call and meet up with her special friend. Within an hour, the two of them were locked in each other's and passed the night away in pleasure.

In the morning, Stephanie made the drive back to Atlanta. They had developed their plan after their love-making and would implement it, starting with the Jacobs woman.

Stephanie also knew Melanie's weakness and would exploit it. Things were going as originally planned. Won't they all be surprised when Stephanie takes matters into her hands? If only they knew?

Linda had an urgent call to make as she wanted company, and if it weren't so late, she'd suggest tonight. Tomorrow afternoon would have to do. She made the call.

"Hi! It's me. I just got home. I'm all right. I have a bunch to tell you, and I need to see you."

"I can come over tonight if you want me to?"

"No, I'm tired and need some sleep. Can you come for lunch tomorrow?"

"I can come earlier if you want?"

"Lunch is better. I'll tell you everything. There are some things you need to know. I'll see you tomorrow."

CHAPTER 28

Stephanie lived in a small two-bedroom townhouse. She didn't need anything larger. The extra bedroom was set up as her office where Stephanie kept her plans laid out on the bed. She'd been living there for two years ever since they found out about Melanie's operation.

She made the call just like she was supposed to. When he answered, he wanted a complete update and as usual skipped the pleasantries. They were always taken care of when they met in person.

"Your plan is going just as you said except for a new wrinkle. Linda Jacobs showed up."

"She's not going to be a problem. In fact, she may just be what we need to speed things up. Has Melanie got any investors yet?"

He was well aware of what Linda could do to their plans, but he could solve that problem. What was important was that Melanie moved forward in getting investors with real money.

"She has three good ones lined up. Two are ready to come up with fifty each and, in a week; the third will be right behind them."

"What about Parker?"

"Melanie wants him to invest $200,000 within a week. She told him, if he does, the other investors will pony up fifty each."

"That's good. 350K should be enough. Once the money is locked in, we'll make our move. I don't want to take any chances on losing it. We don't want to be greedy."

"Whatever you say, it's your plan."

"Does Melanie suspect anything?"

"No. She thinks I can't hear through the office door. The bug we planted is working great."

"Good. Call me when the money is in and watch yourself, Stephanie!"

"Don't worry; I will."

Stephanie was getting tired of being treated like a novice. She'd been around scams all her life. Her mother was a con artist, and Stephanie learned quite a few tricks from her. After she had died, Stephanie was on her own and learned a few of her own.

The first thing she did was create a new identity. No one would recognize Sheryl Wasserman today. A new hairstyle and color job were the first on the list then a fake education. Most of it was false, except for The Woman's School of Business. That was an eight-week course and cost an easy grand, but it was worth it.

The Temp Agency was a good idea. It got her in that Hi-Tech company where she met Alan Davidson. It only took a few times sleeping with him before she managed to convince him to teach her enough about hacking.

When her time was up at the company, she told Alan she was moving out of town and maybe one day they could hook up again. The fool fell for it, and she had one less loose end to concern her.

Her temp agency got her into Melanie's operation. When Melanie offered her a full-time position, she jumped at it. It made his plan that much simpler to execute. Planting the bug was her idea and a stroke of genius as far as she was concerned.

Hacking into Melanie's computer gave her access to all she needed. When it was time to implement the plan, it would be real simple. Another thing Melanie didn't know about her. Melanie thought she was the great scam artist.

Now, she had to figure out a way to play on Melanie's weakness. It will have to be soon because if those potential investors come up with the money, it would be over quick.

CHAPTER 29

Johnny frequently visited the gym and liked to spend time using the weights. He worked hard developing his physique. Johnny enjoyed looking at himself in the mirrors and flexing for the women. Most of them pretended to ignore him, but he knew better because he noticed some looking.

He'd been frequenting the gym ever since he and Melanie moved back to Atlanta. When dressed in street clothes, he looked good. If it weren't for his shyness around women, he'd probably have a girlfriend. In the gym, he seemed more confident, as did most guys.

After showering and dressing, Johnny sat in his car considering what Melanie had told him about today's visitor.

"I don't like it when Melanie gets upset. She's my big sister and has been taking care of me for a long time, but I also look out for her. When Melanie came home tonight, she was very upset. She said Linda wants in on the operation.

"I never liked Linda. She hurt Melanie and almost got her caught the last time they worked together. We had to leave town and stay away too long. Melanie doesn't think I'm capable of taking care of matters, but I sure put a scare into that Parker guy. I don't like him either."

Johnny smiled and waved at two blondes that had exited the gym and passed in front of his car. They ignored him and kept going.

"I wish Melanie hadn't gotten involved with him, not only with this scam but the other way. Now she wants me to watch Stephanie. She wouldn't say why but just to keep an eye on her. I like Stephanie. She doesn't treat me like I'm a fool.

"I'll watch her, but I'm not going to like it. I don't think there is anything to worry about with Stephanie. But Linda is different. If she does anything to hurt Melanie, I'll take care of her. Melanie would never know."

"Stephanie invited me to her place for dinner next Saturday so how can Melanie suggest there's anything wrong. I was surprised when Stephanie asked me, but she makes me feel comfortable which was why I said yes."

Johnny wasn't sure if he would keep his date with Stephanie. Right up until the last minute he was still uncertain, but eventually decided to go.

CHAPTER 30

Porter and Old George had just returned from their morning walk along the beach when Molly's boat pulled up to the dock. He and Old George liked walking along the beach. It made Porter feel rejuvenated.

There was a good bit of beachfront on Porter's Island, and a smart developer could get rich selling home sights if Porter ever decided to unload some of the land. Of course, he'd stipulate that the development had to be far enough away from his cabin, so he still had his privacy.

Porter noticed that Molly hadn't brought anything with her, but she wasn't expected to. He suspected this visit had something to do with things in town.

"Molly! What brings you here? I don't see any provisions on board, so I'm guessing you got something biting your ass."

Molly hitched the boat, walked to Porter and Old George, and gave the dog her hand. Old George licked it and wagged his tail. "Can't you ever say nice to see

you, Molly? Old George does, even if he can't speak." She
waved her hand. "Nice to see you, John Porter!" When she
used his first name, it meant she was annoyed.

"Same here, Molly!"

That was the best she could expect from Porter, but
she'd grown used to it and liked to rib him whenever she
arrived. He'd never change, and Molly didn't want him to.

"I got something to tell you. Let's go inside; it's hot
out here."

"It's not that hot. You're just excited to see me. I got
something to tell you too."

She lifted her eyebrows expecting it would be about sex.

Once inside the cabin, Molly went to the kitchen and
made some iced tea. Something Porter would never think
of doing. He had his beer to cool him off. With the few
ice cubes available, Molly poured herself a glass and asked
if he wanted one.

"Maybe I should. It's a little early for a beer."

"Now, that's a first! Are you sick or something? Since
when do you choose iced tea over a beer?"

"Since what I have to tell you. You want to go first, or
should I?

"I'll go since I made the trip out here. It has to do
with Parker, Barbara, and Linda Jacobs."

"Whose Linda Jacobs again?"

"She's Parker's bank manager. You knew that. Anyway,
Parker has been acting suspiciously as I told you, and get
this! Barbara has been following him to the bank in the

morning and all day long. She suspects he's having an affair with Jacobs, but I don't think that's what's going on.

"Parker and Jacobs used to arrive at the bank early several mornings but not lately. Seems one day, she stormed out of the bank and since then, she gets there after Parker and closer to eight-thirty instead of seven-thirty. I think Barbara has ruled Jacobs out, but I still think there was something there.

"I think Jacobs has something of her own going on that doesn't involve Parker. I just don't know what it is. Jacobs took a trip recently, and I'm guessing she went to Atlanta. Probably to find out what Parker's up to there. I also think Barbara may do the same. She seems obsessed with his doings. Any thoughts?"

Porter mulled it over but had no idea what was happening and didn't care. He was more interested in last night's events and guessed Molly would be too.

"Molly, I don't know what I think, but when you hear what I got to say, you're probably gonna concern yourself less about the Parkers."

"Sounds important, what have you been up to?"

"Yesterday, I saw that boat go by, and I thought it strange they were going by in the evening instead of during the day like they always have. Old George and I decided to take a little boat ride to see what was up."

He was giving the credit to Old George because if it hadn't been for him, they might have missed what happened.

"It's a good thing I brought Old George because once we were around the cove he started acting strange as he has on several occasions.

"As it turns out, the reason he's been acting strangely is because there's been a plane flying low a ways off shore. That's what bothered him. I would have missed the plane if it weren't for him."

Molly was suddenly curious, and Porter's did in fact cause her to forget about the Parkers, and wanted to know more to get that nagging suspicion off her mind.

"So, what was with the plane?"

"Well, we were out without running lights, just to be safe, and when I spotted the plane, I headed for shore. Good thing cause someone else was watching the plane. Remember you had that feeling someone was watching us?

"It was someone on that fancy boat. They were hiding in the marshes, but I caught a reflection from their binoculars. The plane came in low and dropped three packages then took off south. Thirty minutes later, the boat retrieved them and headed north."

"What do you think was in those packages?"

Molly hoped he wouldn't drag it out as she hated long drawn out stories. She just wanted the bottom line quick and easy, no fancy bullshit.

"I'm thinking drugs, and if that's what it is, it's over our heads and out of your jurisdiction. We may have to call in the Coast Guard and the Sheriff. I suspect they'll want to alert DEA. We're out of our league here, Molly!"

"I agree, but do we have enough to go to the Sheriff? He may just ignore us. It's over his head too."

"Then we'll go right to the Coast Guard after we tell him and maybe the DEA. We don't have much choice. So far, they don't know I was there but if they find out we've been snooping, who knows what could happen? They know we've seen them when they go around the cove."

"When do you want to talk to the Sheriff?"

"How bout today? We can take my boat, that way Old George can come. I'm not comfortable leaving him here alone."

"Okay, let's go. Come on, Old George, you're going for a boat ride!"

Old George stood up and wagged his tail as soon as he heard 'boat ride.' If there was one thing he liked better than walks, it was boat trips, especially with Molly along.

The three left after Porter locked the cabin. He usually didn't lock it but for some reason, he decided to. When they reached the dock, Old George jumped into the boat, and Molly was right behind him. Porter untied the boat and joined them. They took off for Blocker's Bluff.

It was going to be a new experience for Porter since he hadn't been in town in a long time. One thing he did know, he didn't want to run into Parker or any of the Town Council. In the event they did, he just might do something Molly would regret. He had promised her if they did run into any of them, he would be civil or just ignore them altogether. It was the best he could do.

But Old George presented a different problem. Old George hated them just as much as Porter did. Porter had no intention of stopping Old George from snapping at them in the event he did, just for kicks.

Molly would be pissed; he was sure, but she'd get a kick out of it just the same.

CHAPTER 31

It was nearly lunchtime on Saturday and Linda wasn't sure how much she wanted to reveal but the more she did, the better she would feel. She wouldn't divulge everything; some things were best left unsaid. Linda was sure her friend and confidant wouldn't condemn her for the past. She poured a glass of wine and waited.

As soon as the doorbell rang, Linda set her glass down and immediately opened it. She had waited impatiently wanting to get it over with, and if all went right, maybe they could finally spend a whole day together.

"I'm here. What's so important?'

Linda didn't return the gleeful greeting. "Come in quickly. Close the door."

"What, no hi or how are you? This must be serious."

"You'd better sit down. You may not like what I have to say."

"At least offer me a glass of wine, since you're having one."

Linda turned and eyed her glass of wine sitting on the kitchen counter.

"Sorry, sit and I'll pour your drink." She took a glass from the cabinet and filled it with wine.

"Thanks now give it to me and don't spare any details. I want to know everything."

Linda picked up her glass of wine, took a sip and said, "I went to Atlanta. That's why I couldn't see you last night or this morning. I knew where Parker's been going, so I went there to confront his girlfriend. She's more than a girlfriend, she's also his partner in the real estate deal involving the land Parker owns west of town. He wants to develop it as a resort."

"But Linda, Parker doesn't have that kind of money! How is he going to finance it?"

"I told you that they're putting together a limited partnership with Tom as the general partner and then selling limited partnerships. The sixty-five thousand we took from the bank was for startup costs. I think he's going to want to invest even more money, and I'm going to have to dig myself in deeper."

"But Linda, this could backfire on both of you. How much more does he want?"

"I don't know, but I suspect I'll find out this week. And there's more. I knew her years ago. She ran a scam, and I got caught up in it. It almost cost me my job, but I was lucky to save my ass.

"The real reason, aside from you, that I took the job with Parker was because I didn't have any choice. I was on thin ice where I worked so when Parker made me a great offer; I jumped at it. I've got skeletons in my closet, and they could come back to haunt me, even more so because of his partner in Atlanta."

Linda searched her friend's face for a reaction but saw a blank page, took a sip of wine and continued.

"If you want to leave now, I wouldn't blame you."

"I'm not going anywhere. We all make mistakes, and I've made some." Linda's smile brightened the room. "So, what are you going to do? How bad is it and who is she anyway?"

"It's terrible, and her name's Melanie Tifton. She used a different name when I knew her, but she's the same Melanie. I think she's pulling a scam on Parker. It's not hard to do, especially with Melanie's background. She's done it before. I'd bet anything that she'll take off with the money and leave him holding the bag, it means I will be too."

"Can you warn him?"

"I could, but then I have to tell him how I came to that conclusion and about my past with Melanie. He may not take it well, and who knows what he'll do. Besides, he has Barbara to deal with."

Linda's friend took a sip of wine and set the glass down.

"You need to know that Barbara has been following Tom around town."

"I know. I've seen Barbara's car near the bank numerous times. Now that you know what's going on, I hope you won't hold it against me. I just wanted to tell you so you could protect yourself. There's no telling what Melanie would do."

"I can take care of myself, but I'm glad you were honest with me. Let's relax and have lunch? We can talk later."

"Lunch sounds good but no more talk. I'd much rather be in your arms."

"I can handle that."

They had lunch and then enjoyed the afternoon together. For now, everything was all right, and Linda was able to relax for a little while. But that wouldn't last long as the week was coming and she would have to face Parker.

CHAPTER 32

Crofton County Sheriff Mackey Stockton was not an easy man to engage in a conversation. He'd been in law enforcement for over forty years and was a throwback from South Carolina's unpleasant past. He didn't tolerate anything. Even his looks were a throwback—big, burly and always puffing on a cigar. He resembled the sheriff in the *Smokey and The Bandit* movie.

Unlike Crofton County, Blocker's Bluff never got caught up in the racial issues of the past sixty years. People in town respected each other's differences and were always there to help each other in time of need.

Molly and Porter didn't know what to expect since she was black, and Stockton had a distaste for black people, and it was evident to everyone in the county.

Porter was a different matter altogether. He and Stockton had locked horns in the past, and Porter had a strong disdain for Stockton. Porter was prepared for the inevitable and expected. Stockton wouldn't pay any attention to Molly and would ignore her.

The two decided that he would do the talking. It didn't matter much because they had already decided they were going to talk to the Coast Guard with or without Stockton's cooperation.

"John Porter! What the hell are you doing here?" Stockton bellowed. "Hell, as I understand it, you've isolated yourself on that island of yours ever since Blocker's Bluff got wise and kicked you out. Smartest thing Parker and the Town Council ever did."

"Fuck you, Stockton. One day, people are going to wise up to you, and you'll find yourself out on your fat ass!"

"Still an asshole, same as always. What brings you to my office? Not looking for a job, are you?" He glanced in Molly's direction. "Chief, if you're smart you'd distance yourself from this asshole. But then, you never was smart when it came to Porter."

"Oh, I'm smart enough and not as dumb as you," Molly replied. "So fuck off Stockton!"

"Come uppity, are you now. Good thing you don't live in Crofton proper or I'd make you regret that remark."

Porter was doing everything he could to control his temper, but Stockton's statement to Molly was pissing him off. For Molly's sake, he'd swallow crow because Stockton would love for Porter to take a swing at him so that he could lock Porter up.

"Look, Stockton, we're not here to make trouble," Porter said. "We want to give you a heads up before we go to the Coast Guard with something. You want to hear it, or are you going to continue being an ass?"

Porter knew Stockton wouldn't be happy that they were going over his head to the Coast Guard. Porter was also confident Stockton wouldn't do anything with their information, but Porter was covering Molly's ass. The Town Council couldn't say she didn't follow protocol.

"What kind of bullshit you got for me, Porter?"

Porter told Stockton what they knew and made sure to say it was Molly's idea to bring it to him. If Stockton did nothing, at least Porter could say he was there as a witness when Stockton received the information. Molly would be the one to talk to the Coast Guard. Molly was sure to be covered on both bases.

"So Sheriff! You gonna do anything?"

"I'll think about it, Porter. No need to go to the Coast Guard. I can take care of it."

"Sure, whatever you say. Come on, Molly, let's go."

"Remember what I said about Porter, Chief."

Molly shot Stockton the bird and she and Porter left.

"Well, that went well. Stockton's still a jerk, and, yeah, a real asshole!"

"That a girl, Molly. You did real good in there."

"So did you. I'm proud of you. It's a good thing we didn't bring Old George in with us. I don't think he would have taken too kindly to Stockton's remarks."

"Old George has a history with Stockton too, and given the chance, he'd take a piece out of his ass, and I'd gladly let him! Come on; let's go see if we can talk to the Coast Guard."

"It might have to wait until Monday; you know the Commander isn't there on weekends unless it's an emergency. I don't want to talk to just anybody."

"You're right, but that means I have to stay in town, or you stay on the island."

"I could make two trips, but I don't like that idea."

"So which is it? My place or yours?"

"Mine, but you'd better be a good boy. What are you going to do about a change of clothes?"

"I got a change on the boat. Let's go get it, and we'll need some food and snacks for Old George."

"We can get them on the way to my place."

They went to his boat, retrieved a change of clothes, and then stopped at Parker's General Store to get food and snacks for Old George.

Miss Mavis was putting baked goods in trays and stopped when they entered.

"Well, I'll be damned!" she exclaimed. "John Porter, how the hell are you? Molly finally got you off that island. It's good to see you, John!"

"Thanks, Miss Mavis. It's good to see you too! Molly's been trying to get me into town, and I finally gave in to her. We need a few things for Old George. You remember him, don't you?"

"Oh, yes! Get what you need. Meantime, I got something for Old George." She grabbed a cookie, bent down and handed to the dog. "Here ya go, boy!"

Old George chomped it down, gave Miss Mavis a kiss, and extended his paw.

They bought what they needed, paid and started out the door.

"Good seeing you, Miss Mavis!"

"You too, John Porter! Don't wait five more years to come back. Molly, you make sure he comes back!"

"I'll be sure of that, Miss Mavis. Take care now!"

On their way out, they noticed Judy Waverly's car go through town and ignored it as Judy often worked on Saturdays.

When they arrived at Molly's, Porter brought the dog food and snacks in and fixed a dish for Old George—but not before giving him a treat.

"Old George is gonna need a walk after dinner, Molly. You up for going with us, or rather not be seen in my company? People will notice."

"After Stockton, I don't care what people notice. Yes, I'll go for a walk with Old George."

"What about me, am I invited?"

"Shut up; you damn fool! I'll fix us some dinner then we can take that walk."

"We could take that walk then go to Parker's Restaurant. I could go for some of Chef Willie's cooking. Not that yours isn't good too."

"What the hell! If you're willing to show your face in town, I'd be glad to be there when people see you. I'd like to see their reaction."

"Okay, Parker's Restaurant and Chef Willie's cooking it is. And screw the townsfolk and the Town Council. I'd be honored to be seen with the Chief of Police!"

"You're crazy, John Porter. You know Chef Willie could give us something for Old George. Why don't we take him?"

When Old George heard Chef Willie's name, he was up and wagging his tail. Hell yeah, he wanted to go to Parker's Restaurant. He hadn't had any of Chef Willie's cooking in a long time.

"Looks like Old George made our decision unanimous. Let's go, Molly!"

"What do we do if Old George runs into any of the Town Council?"

"We'll let Old George decide what he wants to do."

"You know Old George don't like Parker or any of the Town Council," Molly said and then looked down at the dog. "You mind yourself, Old George! And you to Porter."

"Aw shit Molly, you're no fun."

"I mean it, you and Old George better not be bad!"

Porter smiled, Old George barked, and they went to dinner.

CHAPTER 33

When Porter and Molly walked into town, there were only a few people out and about. Surprisingly, they were all very pleasant when they saw Porter and said it was nice to see him; it had been too long. They also commented on his ponytail and liked the new look.

Porter and Molly were pleasantly surprised as they weren't expecting that but these were Blocker's Bluff townsfolk, not the Town Council. There's a big difference between the townsfolk and the Council. The townsfolk were civil, unlike the Town Council.

When they entered the restaurant, Chef Willie was both surprised and excited the three of them had come to the restaurant. He never believed or liked what Parker and the Town Council did to John Porter.

"Well, I'll be! Look who's come to my restaurant? How you doing Chief and you, Old George? You too,

John Porter." Chef Willie said and then pointed to Porter's head. "Nice hairdo! What brings you to town?"

Porter frowned. "Thanks for greeting the dog before me. I'm doing well, Chef Willie. Old George and I have been dying for some good food, and we convinced Molly to bring us here. She said we'd be safe in town with the Chief of Police! You got any catfish tonight and something good for Old George?"

"I got catfish and something special for my favorite deputy. Old George was your deputy, remember?"

"I forgot about that. You got a good memory, Chef Willie."

"Whyn't you call me Willie, Chief?"

"I ain't the Chief no more. Molly is, and I call you Chef out of respect for your cooking."

"You're just like Molly. Both of you are full of shit. No disrespect, Chief."

"None taken, Chef. I'll have the catfish too."

Old George pranced around with excitement. He wanted to know what the special was, but Chef Willie never told him in the past and tonight wouldn't be any different. He gave Old George a leftover short rib.

After dinner, Porter, Molly, and Old George said goodnight to Chef Willie and headed home to Molly's.

CHAPTER 34

Monday morning Parker and Jacobs arrived at the bank simultaneously, and neither exchanged greetings. It wasn't going to be a pleasant encounter as Linda was still agitated from the weekend, but unburdening herself Saturday had helped. Now that some of her past was out, and was accepted unconditionally, she could move on.

Tom Parker was another issue and what he had asked was too much for her. Linda was afraid they were going too far. Melanie must have pushed Parker, or there was something else. Whatever the reason, she wanted more before she agreed to anything.

Once inside the bank, Linda decided to ask how much money Parker wanted.

"How much this time, Tom?"

Parker knew the answer would upset her, but he had too much at stake. Melanie assured him that she had investors for $150,000, and another 200K would seal the deal.

He had an investor willing to put up $500,000 if they had another 200K in hand. It was his investor, and Melanie wouldn't know about him. Parker would have to transfer title to the partnership when his investor was locked in.

"$200,000, Linda. I promise this will tilt the project and get it rolling. I really need your help."

"Are you out of your fucking mind? We can't possibly hide that much."

Parker made the decision to tell her about the investor, as he had no choice if he wanted the 500K.

"We won't have to hide it for long. I've got an investor who will put up $500,000 once the partnership has 350K. The money stays here, and we can always use it to hide the other $200,000 that's going to Atlanta."

Linda decided if she was going to do this, she had to tell Parker about her trip to Atlanta and Melanie. Maybe he'd back out of the whole mess, and they could cover the 69K.

Linda brushed her hair with her hand and said. "Tom, I have to tell you something. I was in Atlanta Friday, and I met with Melanie."

Parker gasped. "You what? Are you out of your mind? Why did you do that?"

"Tom, I know what you and Melanie are doing. If I'm going to put my neck on the line, I needed to find out more about Atlanta and, besides; I know more about Melanie than you do."

"What does that mean?"

"I knew Melanie before coming to work for you. She went by a different name. Melanie's the real reason I took your offer years ago. She and another guy were running a scam, and I got caught up in it. I managed to save my ass, but my career was going down the toilet. You were my lifesaver."

Even though Linda was upset with Parker, she hoped he'd listen to her and use some caution when dealing with Melanie. But she knew he wouldn't, though. Parker was too involved sexually with Melanie for, his own good. At least she was trying to warn him. She owed him that much.

"Melanie and this other guy covered their tracks, and I believe the authorities would love to get their hands on him. Melanie managed to shield her identity and that of her brother's. Trust me, Tom. I believe Melanie is running a scam on you."

Linda warned him, and now the question was what Parker would do. Is he smart enough to cover himself or has Melanie sucked him in too deep? Melanie always used her body to sucker the mark, and Parker was infatuated with hers.

"I don't believe you," Parker replied. "Are you sure it's not jealousy? Come on Linda; you said we were through, and this is my one shot. I need this."

Linda was flabbergasted. "Tom, she has her hooks in you. That's how she operates. If you're that blind, I'm not sure I want to be a part of this anymore."

Parker was too blind to the truth as it pertained to Melanie. Linda had done the best she could, and now it was up to him.

"Look, Linda, this guy I got is for real, and Melanie will never see his money or know about him. I still control title to the land, and Melanie can't get her hands on it. I'll figure out the money situation, but I need this 200K." Parker surprised her and brought his palms together. "I'm begging you, Linda!"

"You're a fool, Tom Parker. I'll help you this time but no more. I mean it. If I have to go to the authorities and plead my case, I will. Melanie is a dangerous woman, and you're going to pay a severe price."

"I hear you, but how do we do this?"

Linda couldn't believe he still wanted to go through with the deal but still laid out a plan for him. Seven mortgage loans of varying amounts so it wouldn't be conspicuous. Parker would approve the loans, and his signature would be on all the paperwork. The borrowers would use the proceeds of the loans to invest in the limited partnership.

Linda's name wouldn't be on any of the documents, so she would be able to fake denial of any knowledge. The biggest problem was the bank didn't have that kind of cash in the vault, and $200,000 represented a sizable portion of the bank's assets. Previously the bank had been cited for retaining excessive money, so Parker had to arrange an account at the Federal Reserve Bank of Atlanta.

They'd have to withdraw funds from the Fed and hope the Office of the Commissioner of Banking and Bank of Nations in Atlanta wouldn't immediately question why the funds went into Strategic Investments account—which was why they used a legitimate use of proceeds for the borrowers.

Linda prepared the paperwork, and Parker funded the loans. Parker would then deliver the bank drafts to Melanie before the week ended. All he had to do now was get Barbara off his back.

When they finished, Parker had to make a call. He talked to Melanie, told her the good news, and what Linda said.

"Tom, ignore her, she's a vindictive bitch. She's the one who ran the scam. I'll tell you all about it the next time you come to Atlanta."

"Okay, we'll talk more when I get there."

"So long, Tom." Melanie slammed the receiver down and shouted, "That bitch!"

Unbeknownst to Melanie, Stephanie was listening to the entire conversation and wasn't pleased with what she heard. Stephanie got up from her desk and went to Melanie's office. She would have to initiate her plan sooner than expected.

Stephanie leaned against the door jam and asked, "What was that all about, Melanie?"

Melanie looked up surprised to see Stephanie standing there.

"Were you listening, Steph?"

"I heard you shout something about that bitch."

"Linda Jacobs told Parker about our history and that I was running a scam on him. I managed to calm him down, and he's bringing 200K here this week. The good thing is now I can get those others to put up their 150K. With 350K, we can attract more investors. But I've got to do something about Jacobs."

Stephanie had plans for Jacobs, and as soon as the $350,000 was in the bank, she'd take care of her. She knew just who to do it and would make the call tonight.

"What are you going to do?"

"I don't know yet, but I'll think of something. That bitch isn't going to screw me again."

While you're thinking, I'll do something, Stephanie told herself. It was all part of the plan that was slowly evolving but soon would escalate.

CHAPTER 35

Porter and Molly had breakfast at Parker's Restaurant before going to meet with the Coast Guard Commander, and hoped by some chance; he might be there.

Unfortunately, the Commander was on vacation and wouldn't be back until Monday. The Chief Warrant Officer on duty asked if he could be of assistance.

Porter wasn't comfortable talking with anyone but the Commander, besides he and the Commander knew each other from when Porter was the Chief of Police.

"That's okay; we can wait. Thanks anyway," Porter said.

"Suit yourself," the officer responded.

"Come on Molly, let's go."

"Why can't we talk to him?" she asked.

"Because I'd rather talk to the Commander. He and I go back a ways. I don't want another Stockton brush off."

"Okay, but what do we do now?"

"How about lunch at Parker's?

"Do you think about anything besides food, John Porter?"

"I think about sex with you all the time, Chief Dickson!"

"Quiet you old fool; someone will hear you." She slapped his arm "You're crazy, John Porter!"

"Crazy in love with you, Chief Dickson!"

Molly smiled. The old fool still loved her, and the feeling was mutual, but she wouldn't admit it. She's kept him on the ropes all these years and planned on keeping him hanging a whole lot longer. Maybe one day, he'd change her mind.

They drove back to town and went to the restaurant. Chef Willie was surprised to see them twice in one day and the third day in a row. Tom Parker who was just finishing lunch wasn't as pleased.

"Morning, Mayor!" Molly said just to be gracious and hoped Porter would ignore Parker.

"Morning to you, Chief!"

Parker ignored Porter but wasn't pleased to see him in town. Parker had other things on his mind, and the last thing he needed was a confrontation with Porter.

Molly was glad both ignored each other, but noticed the unpleasant look on their faces. A look was better than words, she told herself.

"You did the right thing restraining yourself, Porter. We don't need trouble with Parker right now, especially after Stockton yesterday."

"I only restrained myself because of you and Chef Willie. I didn't want any trouble coming back to either of you."

"Thanks, but Chef Willie and I can take care of ourselves. Now tell me more about your relationship with the Coast Guard Commander."

"He and I worked together a number of times when I was the chief. I helped him on a few cases, and he helped me. None of them was anything serious, but the Commander likes to fish, and Porter's Island has some great fishing spots. He visits me occasionally and brings me beer, unlike you."

"How am I supposed to get beer in my boat with everything else I bring you?"

Molly did bring him beer only he didn't realize it when she unpacked his groceries. He would have if he bothered to do it himself. But that would never happen because he's too damn lazy and has Molly.

"Maybe we can get him to visit you and then we can tell him what we think might be going on?"

"That's a good idea. I'll give him a call Monday morning."

CHAPTER 36

Wednesday afternoon, Parker arrived in Atlanta with the $200,000 and gave it to Melanie. She gave him her usual phony smile.

"Thanks, Tom, I'll deposit it in the partnership's account." What Parker didn't know was that there were two accounts.

One account had Parker as General Partner and Melanie as Managing Partner, with both having signing authority. The other account at a different bank had Melanie as the General Partner with the only signing authority and Parker as a Limited Partner. The later one was where she would deposit the money.

"Any chance we can get together this evening, Melanie?"

She grinned and replied, "I don't see why not. I'll see you at your hotel tonight."

Poor Tom Parker, tonight would be the last time he enjoyed Melanie as soon she'd disappear and be $300K richer, but would be kind and leave him with a little something to remember her.

After Parker, left she told Stephanie she had to run to the bank and would be back shortly.

While Melanie was out, Stephanie decided to look at the bank accounts. Johnny was conveniently out of the office. It was easy for her to hack into Melanie's laptop as Melanie still used the same password "Billdeb." After getting the information she needed, Stephanie decided it was a good time to practice her handwriting skills, as she'd need them shortly. She made a quick call and told him about the 200K.

When Melanie returned, she told Stephanie to go ahead and leave as she was too.

Later in Parker's hotel room, Melanie gave him a night to remember. She did everything he asked for even though it was against what little principles she had.

Parker was thoroughly sated, and after Melanie had left, he questioned what Linda had said about her. One thing he was certain of, Barbara didn't give him the pleasure he received from Melanie and what he used to get from Linda.

What Parker didn't know, was that Barbara had followed him to Atlanta and saw Melanie go to his hotel room and was also watching when she left.

Barbara had gotten herself a room in the same hotel.

CHAPTER 37

S aturday night, Stephanie wondered if Johnny was going to show. He was supposed to be there at eight o'clock, and it was already eight-thirty. Maybe she had him figured all wrong. She hoped she hadn't because this was an important part of the plan.

Stephanie lived in a modest two-story, two bedroom townhouse north of downtown with easy access to the airport. The rent was affordable, and it came fully furnished. She had a month left on the lease—which fit into her plans. The first floor housed the living room, the kitchen, a small ding area, and a powder room.

Finally, at 8:45, the doorbell rang. Johnny stood in the doorway dressed in a blue polo shirt and black trousers. She thought he looked pretty good. Maybe he wasn't anything like Melanie had made him out to be. Perhaps when he was away from her, he was a regular guy.

Stephanie had purposefully worn a tight red sheath that revealed plenty of chest and leg as part of her plan to entice him.

"Johnny, I was beginning to think you were going to stand me up. Come in." She turned and walked toward the kitchen allowing him a view of her slender backside.

"I wasn't sure I was going to come."

She stopped and turned. "Why, Johnny?"

"Because I rarely get asked to dinner by a woman as good looking as you."

"Thank you, Johnny, but you're too modest." She winked. "I like you, and I hope you like me."

He smiled. "Oh, I like you."

"Good. Now come, I've got dinner ready. Would you like something to drink?"

"I 'm not a drinker, but I'll take a glass of iced tea."

She had hoped he'd accept wine, but iced tea would work just as well. As she poured the tea, she dropped a little something in it. Not too much. She wanted just enough to relax his inhibitions and lower his guard.

"Here you go, Johnny. Now sit and I'll fix us a plate. Why don't you cut up some cheese for us?" She picked up a knife and handed it to him. "Here, use this."

When he finished slicing the cheese, she retrieved the knife and put it aside for later as she had plans for it.

By the end of dinner, Johnny started to feel the effect of the drug. Stephanie decided to test the waters.

"Johnny. Do you think I'm good looking?"

"Oh, yes, in fact, you're real hot." His face became a shade of pink. "I'm sorry; I didn't mean to say that."

"It's okay, Johnny. I appreciate the compliment. I think you're good looking too."

He blushed again. The conversation was going as Stephanie hoped and decided to go further as she wanted to see how far she could go with him.

"Would you like to kiss me, Johnny?"

"Would it be all right?" He barely got the words out. No woman had ever asked him to kiss her, and he certainly wanted to kiss her.

"I asked you, didn't I?"

He gave her a slight kiss on the lips. Nothing to make a woman feel good about, but she had other ideas.

"Johnny, that's not a real kiss. Try again."

He put his arms around her and placed a long kiss on her mouth. She responded by inserting her tongue deep into his mouth hoping to arouse him.

Suddenly he heard the pa rum pum-pum of the little drummer boy playing on his chest. He'd never been kissed like that before.

She gazed into his eyes and asked, "Would you like to touch me?"

He thought his chest was going to explode and hesitated. Stephanie took his hand, placed it on her breast and held it there. She smiled when his hand started to tremble.

She stood, crooked a finger in her direction, and leaned her head toward the staircase. "Follow me."

He followed her to the bedroom and let her undress him. She was pleased with what she saw and wondered if he was as inexperienced as he acted or faking it. But once in bed, the things he did to her proved he was an expert at lovemaking. She heard Ravel's Bolero playing in her head as he made love to her. Being an expert herself, she made his experience just as memorable. Too bad it would be his first and last time with her.

When they finished making love, she told him how upset Melanie was about the Jacobs woman.

"I don't like that woman, and I don't like how she has Melanie upset. If I knew where she lived, I'd have a talk with her, and I wouldn't be nice!"

Stephanie had hoped it would be his response and knew what to do next.

"I know where she lives, Johnny. But if I tell you, promise me you won't do anything bad?"

"I'll just talk to her. I promise."

She gave him Linda Jacobs's address and again made Johnny promise that he wouldn't do anything bad. He promised, but she didn't care if he broke his promise.

After he left, she carefully retrieved the knife, put it in a bag for another time, and then made the expected call. They'd meet tomorrow at a rest stop off I-75. Stephanie would hand over the knife and then drive back to Atlanta.

The next day, they met, and she delivered the knife. Before she left, she said it was time to deal with Jacobs. It was necessary.

CHAPTER 38

The Coast Guard Commander was pleased to hear from Porter. The two of them hadn't fished together in quite a while, and he was anxious to do so, even though he had just returned from vacation. He didn't get to do much fishing at Disney World with the wife and grandkids.

The Commander was a career serviceman in his fifties with over twenty-five years of active duty. He wasn't the spit and polish type but wore the uniform with pride. He was a seaman at heart—which was why he enlisted right out of the Coast Guard Academy.

When Commander Morris Edison pulled up to the dock, Porter, Molly, and Old George were there to greet him. He expected Porter and the dog but not the Chief of Police. He guessed this wasn't about fishing as soon as he saw them.

"I reckon you didn't invite me here to fish seeing as how the Chief of Police is with you. What's up, Porter?"

"Hitch your boat then follow us up to the cabin, and I'll tell you why I asked you here."

The Commander secured his boat started toward them. Old George walked over and greeted him with a paw and a wagging tail.

"At least Old George knows how to say hello. Not much for you two."

"Sorry. Morning, Commander!"

"Thanks, Chief. You too and even you Porter."

As usual, Porter didn't respond. He never did. It's just how he was, always has been and always will be.

When they were all in the cabin, Molly poured everyone a glass of iced tea and then Porter told the Commander about the boat, the plane, and the packages.

"Sounds like a drug smuggling operation to me," said the Commander. "We've suspected there might be one going on along the coastline, but nobody knows exactly where. You may have stumbled on it. Have you alerted Sheriff Stockton?"

"Yes and the stupid asshole just shrugged us off. Stockton all but dismissed Molly," replied Porter.

"Not surprised. You know Stockton's popularity with the county big wigs is way down. I've heard they'd like to get rid of him. Are you taking this to DEA, or do you want me to?"

"What do you think is best?" asked Porter.

"If it came from me, they'd be more inclined to take it seriously and start something. I'll make sure the DEA knows the tip came from you."

"I'd rather you said it was from Molly. She's the Chief of Police, and it's her jurisdiction. She's supposed to be aware of what's happening. Plus, it would really piss Stockton off."

"I gotcha, Porter." The Commander addressed Molly. "Chief, I'm going to need a statement from you. You okay with that?"

"Sure, but can't you call me Molly like Porter does?"

"Just following protocol and showing respect. I'm not Stockton, and you'll get the credit for this, rightly so!"

"Thanks, I appreciate that."

The Commander went to his boat and came back with his briefcase. He took a formal statement from Molly and had her sign it, and then he got up to leave.

"Still time for some fishing if you're up to it, Mo."

Mo was the nickname the Commander and Porter had agreed on when they went fishing together. Porter wasn't going to let the Commander just up and leave. He was doing a huge favor for Molly and Porter wanted to show him his appreciation.

"I brought my gear and never turn down an opportunity for good fishing. You joining us, Molly?"

"Sure, but since you just called me by my first name I should call you by yours. What is it?"

"Morris, but call me Mo."

"Okay, Mo, let's all go fishing!"

They fished for the better part of the afternoon, and the Commander had a good haul to take home with him. The Commander said his goodbye and left in his boat.

"You know what Porter, it's too late to make the ride back to town, so I'll stay the night." Porter and Old George leaped with joy. "And don't get any ideas, you old fool. We're still on official business. Maybe we'll see that boat go by tonight!"

As they sat on the porch looking out to sea, they saw it go by, and Porter called the Commander to tell him.

CHAPTER 39

Linda was worried about the last transaction, as she was in too deep and had to find a way out. The last time this happened, she ended up in Blocker's Bluff, but where could she go now? She let her desires for Parker get the best of her and was now paying for it.

It was Saturday night, and she wasn't expecting anyone, so when the doorbell rang, she was surprised. They were together last night and agreed that two nights in a row wasn't smart because they didn't want anything to look suspicious. It was how they did it ever since high school.

Linda opened the door and was startled to see who was standing there.

"What do you want? I don't have time to listen to anything you have to say!"

Without warning, the knife plunged into Linda's midsection not once but twice, and she fell back into the apartment.

"Why? What did I do?" she yelled.

There was no answer, and the knife plunged into her again as she fell to the floor. Linda Jacobs' life was coming to an end in a pool of her blood.

The door closed, and Linda was left alone with her fears as darkness overcame her.

"I don't want to die and not alone," were her last words.

But nobody heard her, and Linda would indeed die alone tonight. As her life was fading, she thought of all she was losing.

Yes, she did wrong with Parker, but she had renewed her old love, and now that was gone. Linda wouldn't have to worry anymore about her transgressions at the bank. Maybe she would be forgiven in another world but not tonight.

The killer threw the knife into the azalea bushes at the end of the walkway. Eventually, someone would find it, but that was the way it was intended to happen, and they would be safe.

Linda Jacobs had pissed off the wrong person this time.

Johnny Tifton had parked down the street from Linda's house. As he walked up to her place, he saw some-one leaving, stopped in his tracks, and made sure no one could see him. After the car had left, he went to Linda's door.

It wasn't locked, so he opened it. What he saw frightened him. He turned and ran to his car prepared to drive to Atlanta. Linda Jacobs' dead body wasn't what he expected to see when he arrived at her house.

He was so deep in thought that he didn't notice the old man walking his dog, but the old man saw Johnny's car.

When Johnny went by, Mr. Bradley said to his dog, "Wonder who that was leaving Linda's? He seemed to be in a hurry. Never saw that car before either, and it looked like it had a Georgia license plate!"

Since he was upset, Johnny decided not to drive back to Atlanta. He would have to explain his trip to Melanie, and she wouldn't be happy. He decided to stop at a motel on I-26 for the night and leave in the morning, but he wasn't going to Atlanta. Not yet.

Not only did Johnny not see the old man when he left Linda's, but he also hadn't noticed the car that had been following him since Atlanta.

CHAPTER 40

Tom Parker woke early Monday morning to get to the bank but waited until he was sure Linda was there. There was no point in getting there early any longer. Linda had made it clear that they were over, and she made sure by not arriving at the bank early enough for him to make any advances toward her.

The other reason Parker was up so early was that he didn't want to face Barbara over breakfast. He would eat at the restaurant.

He drove into town, had a peaceful breakfast, said thanks to Chef Willie, and drove to the bank. What he didn't know was that Barbara was following him.

When Parker got to the bank, he saw his two tellers standing outside and suspected something was wrong. He parked his car and walked to the building.

"Why aren't you two inside? The bank opens in a few minutes."

"The door is locked, and we've tried calling Linda, but there wasn't any answer," said Sandy Johnson, the oldest teller.

"What do you mean the door is locked? Where's Linda?"

"That's what I just said! If you want the bank to open, you'd better open it."

Sandy didn't care much for Parker. She'd worked for him since before Linda joined the bank. If Linda hadn't come along as the bank manager, Sandy would have left years ago, in spite of the fact that she was a single mother and needed the job and the income.

"I'll try Linda and then I'll open it," snapped Parker.

Parker called Linda and got no answer, same as Sandy did. What the hell is going on, he asked himself. Linda didn't say anything about taking the day off.

Parker opened the bank, and the tellers went right to work getting ready to open for customers. The two retrieved their carts, counted their money, and put it in their cash drawers. After completing the necessary paperwork, they were ready for business and idle talk.

"What did you do this weekend, Cary?"

"Billy took us all to the beach. We had a great time, and we even picnicked too. What about you?"

"Tommy had a ball game at the ballpark, so I spent time there. I even grilled some chicken yesterday. I almost had a date Saturday night, but the guy backed out on Friday, just my luck."

Tom Parker was upset that Linda wasn't there and that he couldn't get her on the phone. He had no choice but to go to her house and see if she was there.

"You ladies going to be okay without me? I'm going over to Linda's to see if she's there."

"Sure, Mr. Parker, we'll be okay. You go ahead. I hope Linda's all right."

The two of them snickered after Parker left. They both said, "Like, who needs him?"

"Guess Linda and Mr. Parker aren't doing their little thing in the mornings anymore. They think we don't have a clue as to what's been going on," Sandy said.

Cary responded with, "They use his office for more than business matters. I was surprised that Linda's that way, but she always was different back in high school."

Parker and Linda hadn't fooled the two women at all. They'd suspected something was going on for a long time and knew it wasn't banking business.

Parker drove off to Linda's house and was worried as it wasn't like Linda not to show up at the bank without first calling. Almost five years and nothing like this had ever occurred. If she couldn't make it in, she always called him.

Sitting in her car, Barbara wondered what was going on. Why did Tom have to open the bank and where was he going? She followed him carefully to make sure he couldn't see her.

Molly and Porter were just leaving the restaurant when they saw the two cars go by. They were heading back to Porter's Island after she parked her car at the dock.

"Wonder what that's all about?"

"Why? Is that unusual, Molly?"

"Ain't never seen it happen before."

CHAPTER 41

When Parker arrived at Linda's house, he was relieved to see her car in the driveway but concerned why she hadn't answered her phone. He went immediately to the door and rang the bell. When he got no answer, he knocked hard on the door then he tried the doorknob.

The door opened, and Parker stepped inside. What he saw almost made him lose his breakfast. Linda Jacobs was lying in a crimson pool of blood. Parker didn't go any further. He stepped outside and called Chief Dickson.

Molly saw Parker's name on her caller ID, and she answered immediately. Parker had just left town, and she wondered why he was suddenly calling her.

"Mayor Parker, it's Molly. What can I do for you?"

"You'd better get over to Linda Jacobs' house, and you'd best hurry. It's not a pretty sight here."

"I'll be right there," Molly said and hung up.

"What was that all about?" Porter asked.

"Parker said I best get over to Linda Jacobs' house, and it's not a pretty sight there. You coming with me or do you want me to drop you off first?"

"I'll go with you and so will Old George!"

The three of them got in Molly's car and left for Jacob's residence. Her car doesn't have a siren or flashing lights. It looks like an ordinary vehicle except that it says Police on the side. She kept to the speed limit, not knowing if this was an emergency.

When they arrived at the Jacobs' place, Parker was standing outside looking pale as a ghost. Molly knew right away that something was very wrong as she's never seen Parker look the way he did right then, not even that time in the restaurant.

"Mayor Parker, what's wrong?"

"Look for yourself. Linda's inside. What's Porter doing here?"

"He's with me, we have business in town. She looked around. "Porter, follow me, but keep your distance."

Neither Parker nor Porter exchanged glances. There was no love lost between them. Porter walked behind Molly as she requested.

When Molly opened the door and stepped inside, the sight in front of her almost made her sick. She had to quickly back out. Porter took a look since he's had experience with scenes like this from his Vietnam days. He approached carefully.

Linda Jacobs was lying in a large pool of blood and there was splatter on the walls and some of the furniture. It looked like an abstract painting.

"Molly, it looks like someone stabbed her several times, and by the color of all the blood, I'd say she's been dead a while. Don't see any sign of a knife. The killer must have taken it with him or her."

Parker heard Porter and suddenly he thought of Melanie and Barbara. No, it's not possible, he told himself. She said nothing would happen.

"Why do you say him or her? What makes you think it might have been a woman, Porter?"

"Just talking that's all. Don't know who may have done it or why. You know any reason why someone would want to hurt or murder Linda Jacobs?"

"Why are you asking me? Molly, are you going to let him question me like this? I called you, didn't I. Linda didn't show up at the bank, so I came here and that's how I found her. Screw you, Porter!"

Porter wasn't questioning him, but Parker didn't like the idea of Porter being there. He certainly didn't like Porter asking questions, which was why he reacted the way he did.

"Calm down, Mayor. He was just asking a question, and now I'm asking the same thing. Do you know why anyone would want to harm Linda?"

"No I don't, and now I've got a bank to run. If you need me, I'll be at the bank, the restaurant, or at home."

Parker stormed away and drove off knowing he had a call to make. Melanie had better not be behind this, he told himself. Murder was not what Parker wanted any part in, as it would blow the whole deal. Suddenly, he wondered if Linda was right about everything when she told him about Melanie.

Back at Jacob's house, Molly and Porter questioned why Parker was so agitated. They hadn't accused him of anything.

"Boy, he's in a snit. I'd say Barbara might be someone who didn't like Linda. With the way he's been acting the past six months with his trips to Atlanta, my guess is Barbara thinks he's having an affair with Linda or someone in Atlanta."

"Very perceptive, Chief! You've got the makings of a good investigator. You gonna take this or turn it over to Stockton?"

"Damn, I forgot about him. I think I'll run with it some then turn it over to him. Why don't we look around for a murder weapon?"

"Old George can help with that. Let me put some of her blood on my finger then he can sniff it."

Porter carefully put a finger in a spot of blood and got a tiny sample. He made sure he didn't compromise the scene.

Old George didn't need much. He went to the dog, had him sniff, then told him to seek. It was too easy because Old George went right to the azalea bushes at the end of the walkway, stopped in his tracks, and barked.

Porter and Molly approached and, sure enough, right there in the bushes was a knife. It had blood on it, and they were reasonably sure it was Jacob's blood.

"That dog's got some sniffer."

"He does, but that was too easy. Not much thought went into hiding it."

"Got a point there. Let's get this into evidence. Never thought I would ever say something like that. Not here in Blocker's Bluff. Ever been a murder here before, Porter?"

"Maybe in the 1800's, but not as long as I've been around. We got us something new."

They put the knife in a bag and made the call.

Blocker's Bluff didn't have anyone near qualified to be a medical examiner—which meant they would have to call the County Examiner.

They could call the local veterinary, but he wouldn't be of much use, besides this was a criminal investigation. They had no choice but to call Stockton—which they'd regret.

They waited for Stockton and the County Examiner to arrive. She told Stockton they had a murder scene, but he didn't seem that enthused about getting there. Unlike the television shows, the two of them arrived over two hours later and bungled everything.

Stockton walked into the house to check the scene and stepped in Jacobs's blood contaminating the scene. Molly and Porter said nothing. The Examiner was by himself and needed Porter and Stockton to help with the body.

When the Examiner finished after two hours working the scene, they left, and neither of them thanked Molly or Porter.

To his credit, Stockton did manage to get statements from the two of them. He said he would get Parker's another time.

When they were gone, Molly and Porter laughed and so did Old George. It was the funniest thing they'd ever seen.

Porter decided not to go to Porter's Island. He and Molly were going to do some investigating on their own.

Barbara Parker was parked down the street watching everything until Tom left. She knew where he was going, so she decided to go home. She was gone when the Sheriff and the Medical Examiner arrived.

CHAPTER 42

Melanie was feeling good. Once she had all the money in the bank, she would call it quits. She and Johnny would move on and change their identities, but she had to be quick about it. Things were about to change because Parker called and sounded upset.

"Tom, what's up? Hope you had a good weekend."

"What did you do, Melanie? Linda's dead. Murdered in her house. You said you wouldn't do anything bad or was it Johnny?"

Melanie's world started to crumble. Linda's death was a complete surprise, and Parker's reaction was not what she needed now. She had to remain calm and stay focused.

"Wait, Tom, what are you saying? What do you mean Linda's dead?"

"I just left her house. The Chief of Police is there now. Linda didn't open the bank this morning, so I went to her house and discovered her body. It was horrible!"

Melanie's hands started trembling and had to grip the receiver with both. "Tom, listen, I didn't do anything, and I'm positive neither did Johnny. We're not killers. Calm down! We can talk about this when you're unemotional. You're upset now and not making sense. I'll call you later."

Melanie threw the phone against the wall.

"Goddamn it! What the hell's going on? Johnny, I hope you didn't do anything, and where the hell are you?"

Stephanie overheard everything, smiled, and said, "Time to play my role." She got up and went to Melanie's office.

She stood in the doorway, secretly grinned, and asked, "Melanie, why are you so upset?"

Melanie looked up and saw Stephanie. Oh shit, she said to herself. She forgot that Stephanie was at her desk and probably heard everything.

"That was Parker. Linda Jacobs has been murdered in her house. He thinks I may have had something to do with it. You don't know where Johnny is, do you? He didn't come home last night."

"No, Melanie. It's not like he checks in with me. He keeps his own schedule. You want to talk about this?"

"Thanks, but I've got to contact those three investors and get them in here ASAP to make their wire transfers. I'm going to need some help from you, Steph."

"Whatever you need, Melanie."

Melanie made the calls, and the investors said they would be in on Tuesday and Wednesday. They each came separately to the office on the days they selected.

Melanie logged into her account and let each of them see the two hundred thousand deposit. Satisfied, they called their banks and made their transfers.

Periodically, Stephanie came into the office and offered them a cup of coffee or a glass of iced tea. They both chose iced tea, and when Stephanie brought their drinks, she purposefully bent over, so they had a fantastic view of her chest. It helped that she wore a low cut top and no bra. Even Melanie was impressed.

Melanie had her $350,000 in the bank, and Parker didn't have a clue as to where the money went and never would. She was proud of herself and since it was Wednesday, felt the need beat the drum.

"Stephanie, I need to celebrate our accomplishment today. You really helped me out. Those tops you wore were amazing. Did you notice how their eyes were on you and not so much on what they were signing? I owe you big time."

The investor's eyes weren't the only ones on Stephanie. Melanie enjoyed looking also and was always pleased.

Stephanie smiled. "Say, how about dinner at my place tomorrow night? I'll fix you a great meal, and we can toast your success."

"Hey, that sounds like just the thing I need. I haven't shared a meal with anyone other than Parker, Johnny, and those investors." Melanie's eyes sparkled. "Sharing a meal with someone like would be fun. What time?"

"Eight o'clock okay?

"I'll be there!"

And it will be your last meal, Stephanie said to herself, but first, she had to get Johnny out of the picture. He would have to take care of that.

She made the call, and he said he was already taking care of it.

CHAPTER 43

Thursday night, Melanie arrived at Stephanie's townhouse just before eight. She adjusted her low-cut top, tugged at the hem of the tight mini-skirt, and rang the bell. Stephanie opened the door dressed in a black sheath that accentuated her assets, especially those bulging from the top. Melanie had a hard time avoiding them.

Both women's eyes opened wide as they admired each other.

"Damn, you look great, Steph!" Melanie said after catching her breath.

"So do you," Stephanie replied and then gave Melanie time to enjoy the view before inviting her in. "Come in, dinner's ready. I hope you don't mind eating at the kitchen counter."

"That's fine with me as long as I can have a glass of wine."

"I took the liberty of pouring one for each of us unless you prefer something stronger."

"Wine is fine." Melanie followed Stephanie to the kitchen enjoying the view of Stephanie's curves, muscular ass, and her incredibly shapely legs.

Melanie caught her breath, glanced around the apartment, and took notice of how pleasant it looked. It was better than hers, and she wondered how Stephanie could afford the furnishings.

"I like your place, Steph. It's nicely furnished."

"Thanks. It comes with the rent. You didn't think I could afford this stuff on what you pay me, do you?"

"I'm just amazed. You have good taste even if it is rental."

They chatted over a glass of wine and ate dinner. Stephanie had prepared a baked salmon dish with asparagus and red potatoes.

"Dinner was great, Steph. Your culinary skills amaze me."

"Thanks." Stephanie had other skills, but they would wait until later. "Let's sit in the living. We can chat and have some more wine."

Stephanie put the stereo on, found a mood music station, and they moved to the sofa.

Melanie leaned back to enjoy the music, and Stephanie joined her.

"Do you smoke, Melanie?"

"Never tried cigarettes." She sipped her wine and replied, "I can't stand the smell."

"I don't mean cigarettes."

"Oh, that? Yes, once in a while, how about you?"

"Same here, care for one?"

"Sure."

Stephanie set her glass on the end table, reached into it, pulled out a joint, lit it, took a long drag, and then gave it to Melanie.

"Much better than wine," Melanie said and took another long drag.

They shared the joint and then another. When Stephanie felt sure Melanie was high enough, she made her move.

"Have you ever kissed a woman, Melanie?"

Melanie's eyes formed the shape of Oreos, surprised by the question, but she was gloriously high and more than a little aroused by Stephanie. Melanie had experimented some with her college roommate, but she was always on the receiving end. Feeling that she needed a respite, she hoped Stephanie was offering one.

"Yes, a very long time ago. Why do you ask?'

Stephanie inched closer, placed her hand on Melanie's cheek, leaned in and kissed her.

Melanie suddenly felt as though she was leaning against a radiator at a Speedway and hoped Stephanie's kiss meant something sexual was about to happen. She was celebrating the $350,000 and what could be better than to share the bed of this gorgeous woman. She placed her hand on Stephanie's thigh.

Stephanie put her right hand around Melanie's neck and kissed her again, only this time much more passionate. As Melanie returned the kiss, Stephanie used her left hand and plunged the needle into Melanie's neck.

Melanie felt the sting, but it was too late as darkness enveloped her, and she collapsed on the sofa. Melanie Tifton would never see her brother Johnny again, would never sleep with Tom Parker again, would never pull another scam, and would never spend the $350,000. She left the world that morning on Stephanie's sofa.

Stephanie picked up the phone and made the call that he was expecting.

"It's finished," she said.

"Did you have to?"

"No, the bitch was expecting sex, but it wasn't going to happen, and not with me. You need to get here so we can take care of the bitch. I'll go to the office later and make the transfers. Is the brother out of the picture?"

"He's gone. They won't find him for a while."

He arrived within thirty minutes.

"Where did you park?" Stephanie asked.

"A couple of blocks away."

Together, they cleaned the apartment getting rid of all traces of Stephanie and Melanie. Stephanie backed her car out of the garage and then put Melanie's car in. They put Melanie in the trunk; Stephanie got behind the wheel, he got in the passenger's seat, and she drove to where his car was parked.

They drove Melanie's car to Silver Comet Tail and pulled into the parking lot early enough that no joggers had yet to arrive. It would be several days before anyone discovered the car with Melanie in the trunk. Stephanie got in with him, and he drove to a quarter of a mile from her apartment.

Stephanie wore a jogging outfit so it would look like she was out for an early morning run in the event any of her neighbors should happen to see her. Back at the apartment, she finished up the cleaning process, changed clothes, and went to the Office to make the transfers.

After completing the transfers to several different banks, Stephanie put Melanie's laptop in her purse and then made sure there was no evidence that she had ever been in the offices. She sterilized the ladies room and even wiped the elevator buttons.

The building had a modest security system with only a few cameras. They wouldn't be of any use as Stephanie always wore a hat and sunglasses and never looked directly at the cameras, even in the parking garage. She also paid in cash for daily parking down the street so her license plate wouldn't appear anywhere. Stephanie had everything well thought out.

Stephanie drove to the Atlanta Airport, parked in the long-term parking lot, and then caught the shuttle to the terminal. Eventually, someone would find the car, but the registration and license plate belonged to an eighty-three-year-old woman who died two years earlier.

Her sixty-three-year-old son, whose eyesight was less than it used to be, would remember only the cute redhead with the big bazookas who had purchased it a few years ago. Stephanie had covered her tracks well and had almost all the loose ends tied up.

She wasn't worried about the investors since they never looked at her face; their eyes were always focused a foot lower. Whenever they arrived, Stephanie made sure she was leaning forward at her desk affording them a bird's eye view of her assets. The distraction always worked.

Stephanie met him in the terminal. They boarded their flight and were on their way to the Bahamas as Mr. and Mrs. Jansen.

Four days prior, Johnny Tifton was distraught over seeing Linda's body and had to drive around for a few days to erase the image. He knew Melanie would think he killed Linda. If he stayed away long enough, she might not be as mad, plus he would have several motel receipts to prove he wasn't anywhere near Blocker's Bluff.

What Johnny didn't know was that there was a car following him since he left Atlanta. The car was far enough back as the driver had attached a tracking device to Johnny's car.

When Johnny stopped at the third motel in South Carolina, he paid for his room, parked his car, and then went to his designated room. He opened the door and just as he was about to enter, he felt the sting from a needle. It was over in seconds. Johnny Tifton left the world alone in a Motel 6 room.

Like his sister, he would never pull another con. Where he was going, he wouldn't need a workout at the gym, and would no longer have to worry about his shyness around women. He also didn't have to worry about what Melanie would think.

Johnny was laid to rest on the bed, the door was closed and locked, the do not disturb sign placed on the door-knob, and the keys thrown in a waste receptacle.

CHAPTER 44

Parker was still upset over finding Linda's body and the questioning by Molly and Porter. Melanie had assured him that she had nothing to do with Linda's death but he had his suspicions. Johnny was capable of anything, maybe he was behind it, but he wouldn't do anything without Melanie's approval.

He was standing in the kitchen having a drink, his second one when Barbara approached him.

"What are you going to do now that Linda is gone? Were you fucking her, Tom?"

Parker was surprised by the question, and it annoyed him that she asked. He was even more annoyed at her aggressive tone.

"What's with you, Barbara? Linda's dead. Can't you give it a rest?"

"You don't seem to be able to, Tom. How many drinks does that make?"

She was pressuring him and thoroughly enjoying it.

"It's my second. You know, Barbara, you've become a mean bitch. Sometimes, I can't believe you're the cheerleader I once fell in love with!"

The remark touched a nerve and triggered an angry response that she no longer could contain.

"You son of a bitch! If you had learned to keep your dick in your pants, maybe things would have been different. You're the one who had the affairs. Yes, Tom, I know all about them."

"You're fucking crazy, Barbara! Take a look in the mirror. That's why I had affairs. If you want to blame anyone, blame yourself."

He finally said what he'd wanted to say for a long time, and he meant it. It wasn't just the kids that made him stay with her. He needed the appearance.

Again his remark hit Barbara hard, and she started to lose control. If he said anything more, he'd regret it.

"Don't push me, Tom. I'm tired of your vicious remarks."

"Screw you, Barbara!"

That was it. Barbara had enough. She'd reached her limit of self-control.

Parker turned to get another drink, and that's when he heard the expletives from his wife that he'd never heard before.

"Fuck you, Tom Parker! You son of a bitch!"

Volcano Barbara suddenly erupted. She picked up the Oriental vase her parents had brought in Hong Kong and walked up behind him. The first blow hit him on the back of his head. He turned to face her as the second blow hit him in the face. He started to lose consciousness as the third blow shattered the vase.

As Barbara watched the shock in his eyes, she scored a lucky bullseye, hitting him dead center of the juggler. As the crimson tide spilled onto her hand, Parker made a futile attempt to reach up and grab his neck after Barbara removed the shard. As he slipped to the floor, his head hit the counter top and cracked his skull. Barbara yelled, "Yippee!" And then she fired another salvo. "I hope you rot in hell, Tom!"

Tom Parker's life was over. He would never see his deal come to fruition and wouldn't see his children graduate from college. Parker would never again shun his wife in their bed. He was paying for his faults.

Barbara felt no remorse for her actions and finally succeeded in doing what she'd wanted to do for a very long while.

Now she had things to do. She went to her bedroom closet and retrieved the boxes she'd hidden away long ago. Two boxes contained wigs, the third contained cash she'd been secretly saving plus some passports and other identification. Barbara packed a small traveling bag, left the house, and got in her car.

Barbara Parker left Blocker's Bluff for good. She would miss her children, as she would never see them again, but they were grown and could take care of themselves. They each had a trust fund that would get them through college. After that, they had to fend for themselves.

Her parents weren't too keen on her marrying Tom Parker, but they loved their daughter, so they said nothing. They would be pleased that she was no longer strapped to him but not in this manner. Her parents were the ones who set up the children's trust funds and, for that, they would be glad they had.

It didn't matter because Barbara was on her way to her new life with her sister. Tom Parker and her family would be a forgotten memory to her.

She drove to Charleston where she parked her car in a 24-Hour Barbeque Spot restaurant's parking lot, went into the restaurant's bathroom, put one of the wigs on, left the restaurant and nobody noticed her different appearance.

Next, Barbara retrieved her bag and the box with another wig and then called a taxi. When the taxi arrived, she told the driver that her husband left her stranded and would he take to a car rental agency?

The taxi took her to the nearest Easy Car Rental where she rented a car with a one-way drive to Charlotte. She had several false ID's and pre-paid credit cards.

Mary Bennett gave her credit card and license to the attendant, located her car, and then drove to Charlotte. In Charlotte, Mary Bennett boarded her flight. When the plane was in the air, she ordered a cocktail then sat back and enjoyed the flight that would eventually get her to Aruba and the start of her brand new life. Barbara Parker would cease to exist, and her whereabouts would become a mystery.

Their plan was hatched months ago during a rendezvous at the Motel 6 off I-95. When she learned of Melanie's scheme with Tom, she immediately called Barbara and said they needed to talk. Barbara was furious and agreed to the plan as soon as she heard it.

Barbara's job was to step up the pressure on Tom, and she would take care of the technical aspects in Atlanta. Since she had the know-how, the sophisticated part of their plan belonged to her.

Everything had gone as anticipated and soon, they would be basking in the sunlight, $350,000 richer.

CHAPTER 45

Off the coast of Porter's Island, a fifty-foot fishing trawler anchored fifty miles out from the island. On board were Porter, Molly, Old George, several DEA officers, and Coast Guard personnel.

The trawler had been there for several days, and the only ones visible on board were four fishermen who seemed like they were working the lines. Inside the main cabin, Commander Edison had eyes peeled on the shoreline. He spotted the boat within minutes hidden in the marshes just like Porter said it would.

Porter was along to point out the location, and Molly was there as a courtesy. Old George was on board because of his ability to sense the plane.

Old George started acting as he did the other times when he detected the plane. Commander Edison searched the skies and saw the plane coming in from the south. He radioed Jacksonville and put them on alert.

"Good dog, Old George!" the Commander said and reached down to pet him. "We may have to put you in for a Coast Guard commendation!" Old George wagged his tail and gave the Commander a look of excitement.

As the plane made its run, Commander Edison radioed Jacksonville and told them to scramble the aircraft.

Just before reaching its drop sight, the pilot radioed the boat and asked about the trawler. The woman said it was no problem; the trawler had been there when they arrived, and those on board were bringing in their nets and throwing them back into the sea. As best they could tell from their hiding spot, it was just a fishing trawler, and besides, it's nighttime so whoever is on board won't be able to see them. The pilot dropped the three packages.

USCG Sector Jacksonville was on alert for this operation. As soon as they got the go ahead, the aircraft took off from the Mayport, Florida base. It arrived within twenty-five minutes equipped with a radar guidance system to track the plane's movements from afar. When the plane made its drop and headed south again, the Coast Guard aircraft was on its tail.

When the plane reached its destination at Opa-Locka Airport in Miami, a call was placed to DEA enforcement personnel awaiting instructions. They arrested the pilot and confiscated the plane. The first phase of the operation went as planned.

The Coast Guard aircraft made a turn and headed north again. There was just enough time, as the boat would wait thirty minutes to retrieve the packages. When the boat came out of the marshes, Commander Edison radioed the plane.

Everyone on the trawler waited with anticipation. As the boat headed north, Commander Edison radioed DEA personnel waiting on two seemingly small pleasure craft that were hiding in the marshes at the tip of the island. Both were awaiting orders to follow the fancy boat when it headed north at a good distance back. They were in constant contact with the Coast Guard aircraft.

The Coast Guard aircraft pinged the boat and followed it to its destination. The pilot radioed the two pleasure crafts, and ahead to the DEA personnel that were located at several locations to assure that they would be in position when the boat docked.

Fortunately, the boat chose the one near Long Beach, Virginia. Within minutes of docking, DEA agents swarmed it. In custody, the man and woman didn't waste much time asking for a plea deal that included witness protection.

With the information the DEA obtained from the couple and the pilot, they were able to bring down a drug operation that stretched from Virginia to Connecticut. It also put a huge dent in a Columbia Cartel's operation.

The DEA and the Coast Guard sent special letters of thanks to Porter and Molly with an extra special one to Molly thanking her for uncovering the operation that led to the arrests.

To the Crofton County Commission, both agencies sent letters asking why Sheriff Stockton never notified them when he was alerted by Chief of Police Molly Dickson of Blocker's Bluff.

When Stockton came up for reelection, he no longer had the support of some prominent South Carolina Democrats as well as the County Commissioners. He was voted out of office unanimously, and replaced by one of his deputies who ran against him at the urging of the commissioners. There was no love lost between the Sheriff and the deputy.

Several months later, Stockton's body was found in a ditch on a dirt road at the western edge of the county. The investigation of his death lasted three weeks and was considered a possible suicide, as it appeared he lost control of the car and landed in the ditch.

Stockton was cremated and his ashes accidentally thrown in the dumpster outside the crematorium. They were never discovered missing. Nobody in Crofton County cared much.

Commander Edison personally dropped Porter, Molly, and Old George at Porter's dock. He thanked them and said he hoped he would be invited back soon for some fishing.

CHAPTER 46

Monday morning, Porter, Molly, and Old George were just finishing breakfast at Parker's Restaurant when Sandy Johnson and Carey Parks, the tellers from the bank, came in. They spotted Chief Dickson and walked over to her.

Molly wondered why they were at the restaurant and not at the bank.

"Sandy, why aren't you and Carey at the bank?" Molly asked.

Sandy did all the talking.

"There's a problem there. Mr. Parker hasn't arrived yet to open the bank, and neither of us can open it. We've tried calling him on his cell and at home, but there's no answer. After what happened to Linda, we're worried."

Molly was alarmed too. Tom Parker would never forget to open the bank, especially since Linda's death.

"Let me try him. If I get no answer, I'll go to his house. Mrs. Parker should have answered if she's home."

Porter said nothing, but he gave Molly an, uh, oh look.

"I didn't get an answer either. You ladies wait here. Porter and I will check Parker's house."

"We're not going anywhere, but since we're here, we'll have coffee and pie."

Porter, Molly, and Old George drove to Parker's house. When they arrived, Parker's car was in the driveway, but there was no sign of Barbara's.

"I don't like the looks of this, Porter," said Molly. "This doesn't look good."

"I agree, let's see what's up," He replied.

The three approached the front door, and Molly rang the bell. No one answered, but suddenly Old George started acting agitated. Porter knew that meant trouble.

"Molly, Old George is acting like something's wrong. Try the door!"

She tried the door, but it was locked. She pounded on it several times and then called Tom and Barbara's names. Still, she got no answer.

Without warning, Porter kicked the door open.

"What the hell did you do that for?"

"Because there's something wrong. We've already had one murder. Let's hope we don't have three. Go on in, and I'll follow you like last time."

They entered the house and looked around. Next, they moved to the kitchen and discovered Parker's body.

"Shit! Here we go again," exclaimed Molly. "Two murders in this little town within less than two weeks and we don't know if we have three yet."

"Molly, I'll check their bedroom and see if there's any sign of Barbara or what may have happened. You might want to take a picture of whatever's broken on the floor."

Molly took a picture while Porter checked the bedroom.

"There's no sign of anything in there, and the bed didn't look like anyone had slept in it."

"Where the hell could she be, and is she alive?"

"Maybe she's running. She's been acting strange and following Parker around. Could be she finally had enough of his wandering ways and snapped. It is known to happen, Molly."

"In mystery novels, yes. But in Blocker's Bluff? The only murder we've ever had was someone running over an armadillo crossing the road."

"You're not gonna call Stockton, are you? Remember what happened last time?"

"I'm not going to go through that again. Maybe we should call the State Police? You got any contacts there?"

"No, but Commander Edison does, and he owes us a favor," replied Porter.

"Call him then!"

Porter called him, and Edison said he had a contact, and would call him.

"Expect a call shortly, Porter and I agree that Molly shouldn't call Stockton."

Within minutes, Porter received a call from a Sergeant Vickers of the Homicide Investigations Sector of the South Carolina Law Enforcement Division in Columbia. Vickers said he'd have a forensic team and some investigators there in less than two hours. He also told them to secure the scene and wait for him.

Within an hour and a half, Vickers and his team were there and took control of the scene. Porter and Molly told him about the Jacobs murder.

Vickers was a savvy law enforcement officer with twenty years of experience and well aware of Molly's background with the Highway Patrol. Like Porter, he also had no use for Sheriff Stockton.

"Chief, no one has contacted the State about any Jacob's murder. Did you report it to Stockton?

"I did, and he took over the investigation. I thought he would have notified you guys.

"Not the first time Stockton has fucked up a criminal investigation! Sorry Chief, excuse the language. I get annoyed whenever Stockton is involved."

"That makes three of us. Sorry four of us." Molly replied. "That's Old George, and he's the one who sensed something was wrong when we got here."

"Is he yours, Chief or yours Porter? Either way, you've got one hell of a detective there."

When Old George heard the comment, he walked up to Vickers and extended a paw.

"Well, I'll be damned!" said Vickers.

With the crime scene in real hands, Porter and Molly left to do some investigating on their own. Barbara Parker was still missing, and Vickers would investigate that also.

Molly wanted to ask some of Linda Jacobs' neighbors some questions. She was sure Stockton had never bothered to.

First, she had to call the restaurant and tell Sandy and Carey the bad news and tell them to go home.

The situation was getting to be some mess, and it wouldn't be long before this little town was all over the news. Reporters will eat this up since it's not every day that a double murder, possibly triple, occurs there, and there's also the possibility of a kidnapping of the Mayor's wife.

CHAPTER 47

When Molly and Porter pulled into the Jacobs' neighborhood, they decided to knock on some doors together. Since she's the Chief of Police, it would seem more official.

They knocked on a few doors, but nobody saw anything nor heard anything the night of Linda's murder. They were just about to leave when Old Man Nickson walked up to them.

"Howdy, Chief! You investigating the Jacobs woman's murder? That Stockton idiot didn't do anything after you left!"

"I sure am, Mr. Nickson. You see anything that night?"

"Didn't see anything at her house, but when I was leaving to walk the dog, I saw a car go by heading in the opposite direction. Couldn't see much, but I did notice it seemed to have a Georgia license plate. Why would someone from Georgia be in this neighborhood?"

"Don't know, Mr. Nickson, but thanks for the information."

"Hope it's useful, Chief."

"We'll find out. You take care now."

"You too, Chief and you too, John Porter! Nice to see you finally came off that island of yours. You should do it more often. I'm sure Molly would like that."

"Thank you, sir. I'll take your advice."

"Old George, that's his name, right? You take care too."

Old George wagged his tail, grateful for the attention.

Molly called Sergeant Vickers and gave him the information. He thanked her and said he would let her know what becomes of the investigation. He owed her that much.

CHAPTER 48

The Palace Hotel, located on Paradise Island in the Bahamas, was often a destination for foreign travelers. The hotel staff honored the privacy of its visitors and in return, was rewarded with generous gratuities.

Mr. and Mrs. Jansen checked into their hotel room. Booked for only a week and then they were moving on to another island in the Bahamas. When their belongings were in the closet, they decided it was time to catch up on what they both had been missing.

They quickly undressed, climbed into bed, took each other with a vengeance to make up for lost time, and to forget Melanie. When it was over, they fell asleep beside each other.

Finally, their plan had come to fruition, and soon they'd enjoy the monetary gift from Melanie and Parker. It was their ultimate scam of a scam.

In the morning, they ordered breakfast in bed. Later Mrs. Jansen showered, got dressed, and said she was going shopping for some clothes, as she only brought a small carry-on because they didn't want to check any luggage. He'd go shopping later for Bermuda shorts and t-shirts.

Mrs. Jansen purchased a few outfits and a slightly larger carry-on bag. She also bought two wigs and managed to get both in the bag. Next, she went to the bank, withdrew some funds, and arranged a wire transfer of the remainder to a bank account in Aruba opened by her sister.

When she returned to the hotel, he was taking a nap. When he woke, he went to do his shopping. He purchased a few articles of clothing and stopped for a drink at a local Tiki bar where he enjoyed himself watching the women in their little bikinis.

The Jansens went for dinner in the hotel dining room and enjoyed a few drinks in the bar. They were still feeling the effects of the previous day's plane trip and their antics in bed the night before, so they decided to turn in early. But first, he made love to her again.

The Jansens fell asleep and in the early morning Mrs. Jansen rolled over and inserted the needle. He never woke up and Mr. Jansen, a.k.a Bill McPayne would never pull another con again. McPayne wasn't part of the actual plan—he just thought he was. He was the victim of his last con.

Mrs. Jansen wiped all evidence of her from the room. She dressed, closed the door, put the do-not-disturb sign on it, and then went to the front desk.

A different clerk was on duty then when they checked in. The clerk was a nice young man and took greeting guests as a serious matter. His only fault was he never made eye contact.

"Good morning! How can I help you?"

Mrs. Jansen noted the lack of eye contact. His eyes were focused somewhere else, which was fine with her.

"Good morning to you. Looks like another nice day" she said.

"It's always a beautiful day in the Bahamas!" It was his standard cliché, which she found rather amusing.

"I'm Mrs. Jansen in room 436. I'm going shopping, and my husband is sleeping in. I put the do-not-disturb-sign out, so I would appreciate it if you would tell the cleaning staff to skip our room for today."

"No problem. I'll take care of it. Enjoy your shopping spree!"

"Thanks!"

Mrs. Jansen walked to the hotel next door, found the ladies room, changed outfits, put on one of the wigs, and a different pair of sunglasses. Satisfied with her appearance, she left the ladies room and asked the bell clerk where she could get a taxi. He told her there's always one parked at one of the hotels, but he could call her one.

"Thank you! I'm sure I'll locate one," Mrs. Jansen replied.

Mrs. Jansen left the hotel and walked over to the garbage dumpster. Nobody noticed her remove the package from her bag and drop it in. Next, she walked over to where a taxi was parked and asked the driver to take her to the airport.

At the airport, Rosalyn Bennett purchased a one-way ticket to Aruba, boarded the plane, sat back in her seat, and enjoyed the flight.

So far, everything was going as expected. Bill McPayne was gone as was Melanie, Johnny Tifton, Linda Jacobs, and Tom Parker. They had covered their tracks well, and soon, she would be with her sister Mary.

CHAPTER 49

When Judy Waverly heard about Tom Parker's murder and that Barbara was missing, she became upset and could hardly control herself. First Linda, then Tom, and now her best friend, Barbara, was missing.

Even though she made a promise, Judy knew she had to tell what she knew. There was no longer any reason to keep their secret and decided to talk to Molly. Judy felt confident Molly would understand and wouldn't judge her as they'd known each other a long time.

Molly, Porter, and Old George were sitting in her office mulling over what they knew about the cases so far. Where was Barbara Parker was the ultimate question, and could she have killed Tom? And who killed Linda Jacobs? Could it have been the same person— and if so, why? That was the unanswered question. Why?

As they pondered the why, Judy Waverly came into the office looking a bit weary. "Good morning, Molly! John Porter, it's good to see you in town."

"Thanks, Judy, it's good to see you. You here to see Molly?" Porter asked.

"Yes, I am. I have something to tell Molly. It has to do with Linda Jacobs and Tom Parker. Maybe even Barbara."

Molly was rubbing Old George's back, but when Judy said she was there about the cases, it caught her attention. It's rare that Judy ever comes into the police station.

"Porter, get her a chair."

He got a chair for Judy, offered it to her, and then sat back down, glanced at Molly letting her know that she should ask the questions.

"What do you have to tell us, Judy?" Molly asked.

"I think I know who killed Linda and possibly Tom."

Molly and Porter's eyelids hiked with interest, and they moved their chairs closer to Judy. Old George's ears perked up—he was also interested.

Judy nervously alternated rubbing the back of her hands with her fingers. "Linda told me some things in confidence, but there's no longer a reason for me to keep her secret. I couldn't live with myself if I withheld information that might catch her killer."

Molly looked at Porter. He raised his eyebrows, and his face registered skepticism. She felt the same and guessed he was thinking as she was, that this was getting to be a doozy of a mystery and this kind of stuff only happened in the movies.

"What information could Linda have shared with you that was a secret and why you?" Molly asked, but she was puzzled about what Judy knew.

Judy hoped that Molly and Porter wouldn't condemn her, but knew she had to tell them—she'd kept the secret far too long.

"Linda and I have been close ever since high school. When she moved back to town we reconnected."

Molly knew Judy and Barbara were close friends—but not Linda and Judy.

"I didn't know you two were friends, Judy. How close were the two of you?"

Judy suddenly stood and turned to leave. Molly looked at Porter, and he shrugged his shoulders. Judy turned around and sat back down.

"Let's just say very and spare me the embarrassment of the details. Please, Molly!"

Porter and Molly wondered what she meant by very close, but ignored it. It was Molly's case, and it was best he let the woman open up to another woman.

"Okay, Judy. I won't embarrass you. Just tell me what you know."

Judy's hands trembled.

"Thank you, Molly and you too, John for not saying anything." Porter ran two fingers across his lips, signaling they were sealed. "What I have to tell you will shock you, and if it comes out, it won't be good for this town. Linda and Tom were having an affair, but she broke it off months ago. I'm sure you're not surprised at that, but he was also having an affair with a woman in Atlanta."

Molly and Porter weren't surprised as they suspected such.

"Judy, I surmised that, but who is the woman in Atlanta?"

"Her name is Melanie Tifton. She and Tom were working on a real estate deal involving the acreage he owns west of town. It included quite a bit of money. Linda said $850,000."

Molly almost flipped backward, but Porter remained upright in his chair.

"Tom didn't have that kind of money, Judy. Where was he getting it from?"

"This is the awful part. First, mind if I have some coffee?"

"Sure, would you like Porter to get it for you?"

"No thanks, I'll get it myself." She walked to the coffee pot, poured a cup, returned, sat down, took a sip, and continued. "Tom was embezzling money from the bank and made Linda help him. She didn't want to at first but after she had learned that he'd already had taken $15,000, she felt by knowing and doing nothing about it, she was complicit."

Porter glanced at Molly and decided to interject.

"Judy, why didn't Linda go to the authorities right away or come to Molly? She might have been able to exonerate herself instead of becoming complicit?"

Molly's look told him to butt out, but since his question made sense, she bit her lip and said nothing.

"Because Linda had embezzled bank funds before. It wasn't much but still she was afraid if she turned Tom in, the authorities would eventually discover what she did."

Molly and Porter were shocked by Judy's revelation. Things like this don't happen in a place like Blocker's Bluff. In a movie script or fiction novel maybe—but not here in this town.

Linda continued. "She told me why she did it, and that was why she went along with Tom. At first, it was $65,000, but then he wanted another 250,000. Linda was afraid she was already in too deep and didn't know what to do, so she went along. She even came up with the plan to hide the transactions. They created some false mortgages."

"Judy, where did the money go?"

Molly had a bad feeling about what the answer might be and what Judy meant about it not being good for the town.

"It went to the Tifton woman in Atlanta. Linda went there to confront her when Tom told her what they were doing with the money. Apparently, Linda knew the woman from her past."

Molly and Porter shook their heads.

"What do you mean her past?" Molly asked. "I thought Linda had worked for another bank before Tom hired her?"

"She did, but that was a long time ago," answered Judy. "She got mixed up with the Tifton woman and almost lost her job and career. Tifton was a con artist and running a scam at the time. Linda managed to walk away without any legal trouble but needed to find a new opportunity. That's when Tom came along."

Molly and Porter wondered what else Judy would spring on them?

Judy nervously rubbed her right arm and continued, "Linda discovered that the Tifton woman was pulling another scam, and Tom was her mark. That's how Linda explained it. She tried to tell Tom, but he wouldn't listen to her. Linda also said she wouldn't help him anymore, and was considering going to the authorities."

Molly and Porter weren't surprised that Parker ignored the warning. Parker was too stupid and greedy to do otherwise. They listened as Judy continued with her story.

"She promised me that she'd keep my name out of the whole mess because by telling me I was also complicit. Linda made me promise never to say anything, but I can't keep her secret anymore, even if it causes me trouble. Molly, I think that may be why she was killed and might be why Tom was too. If I were you, I'd want to know what's going on in Atlanta!"

Molly knew this information shed serious light on the situation, and the case was now over her head and Porter's too. She'd have to go to the State authorities, probably both in Georgia and South Carolina. It could even involve the FBI and would turn the town upside down, but she had no choice and knew Porter would agree with her.

"Judy, is there anything more you can tell us?" Molly asked.

"I think I've pretty much told you all I know. Am I going to be in trouble?"

"It's a possibility, but we'll try our best to keep your involvement to a minimum. I appreciate your honesty, Judy. As for the other thing, that's between the three of us."

"Thanks, Molly! I appreciate it. If I need to get a lawyer, will you let me know?"

"If it's necessary, I'll let you know. You have any idea about Barbara?"

"No, and I'm worried." Judy's lips pursed. "You don't think?"

"Anything's possible," replied Molly.

"She was upset with Tom, but I don't think she—" Judy didn't know just how upset she was and that Barbara followed Parker to Atlanta. "No, she wouldn't."

"Right now she's a missing person and a person of interest. We'll let you know if we learn anything."

Judy brushed the back of her head and then departed leaving Molly and Porter with their discovery and what their next move should be.

"What do you think? What do we do now?"

"What we have to do, Molly! Call the authorities. Let's start with Vickers and let him take it from there. I'm curious about Atlanta, though. One thing's certain; we don't want Stockton involved."

"I agree. I'll call Vickers. Won't he be surprised?"

Molly placed the call and within an hour and a half, Vickers was in her office. She and Porter told him everything that Judy said and asked if it was possible to spare the woman from any legal trouble?

Vickers said it might be possible since she came forward with the information voluntarily, and it may help solve two murders and a money scam that just might involve the FBI.

"I'll do the best I can, Molly, but I'm not sure about the FBI, sometimes they can be complete assholes in matters like this."

"Thanks, just do the best you can. Judy's a decent person, and I'd like to keep her out of trouble."

Vickers made some calls and said he would like to talk to the Waverly woman. Molly called Judy and told her Vickers was coming to speak with her, but made no promises.

"Thanks, Molly, wish me luck," Judy replied and waited nervously for Vickers.

Molly hoped she had done the right thing and that Judy would be safe.

"You think she has a chance, Vickers?" Molly asked.

Vickers tilted his head sideways. "I'll let you know what develops with her as a professional courtesy to you." Vickers then said goodbye and left to speak with Judy.

Molly and Porter sat in silence pondering Judy's remarks.

"That's a hell of a mess to absorb. I sure hope Judy fares well in this. Parker ruined many lives with his greed, and we still can't account for Barbara. At least Vickers isn't like Stockton, thank goodness."

After their last encounter with Stockton, they didn't want to go through another. Porter knew he wouldn't be able to control his temper. Molly probably couldn't either.

"You're right, but this town is going to suffer because of this. Parker not only ruined his life and others but has also hurt Blocker's Bluff. The bank most likely will go under, folks here are sure suffer, and they don't deserve to!"

"Let's go fishing and put this thing out of our minds for a while, Molly."

CHAPTER 50

A t the Grand Hotel in Palm Beach, Aruba, Mary
Bennett checked in at the front desk, received her
room key, told the clerk that her sister would be
joining her in a few days, and asked to have a key waiting
for her when she arrived. The clerk was very accommodating, said no problem, and then wished her a pleasant stay.

After Mary Bennett had settled in her room, she went
shopping to purchase some clothing and a pair of wigs.
The next day she went to one of the banks that accom-
modated foreigners and opened an account in the name of
Patricia and Louise Connolly.

She told the bank officer to expect a money transfer,
and when her sister arrived, she would sign the signature
card. The bank officer asked how much the money transfer
would be, but Patricia wasn't sure, except that it would be
in the five figures.

With her banking done, she did some window-shop-
ping, went back to the hotel, changed into a swimsuit,

and sat by the pool. Everything was going as planned and she couldn't wait until her sister arrived.

Two days later, Rosalyn Bennett's plane touched down at the Aruba airport. After debarking, she caught a cab to the Grand Hotel, she went to the front desk, told the clerk who she was, and asked for her room key.

"Do you know if my sister is in the room?" she asked.

"I'm not certain, but I can call and find out if you'd like?"

"That's okay. I'd like to surprise her since we haven't seen each other in a while."

"We hope you enjoy your stay, Ms. Bennett!"

"Thank you. I will."

Rosalyn Bennett went to her room, inserted her room key, and entered. Mary wasn't there. Rosalyn thought she might be shopping. Since Rosalyn had some banking to do, she walked to the bank, informed the bank officer that she was Louise Connolly, and was there to sign a signature card.

"We've been expecting you, Miss Connolly," said the male bank officer and never looked at her face.

Louise signed the card and asked if the transfer of funds had come in.

"Yes, ma'am it has," the officer replied and again didn't bother to look at her face.

Louise Connolly left the bank, but before returning to the hotel, she checked on the charter boat that was pre-arranged to take Doris Mitchell and her sister, Rebecca, to the States as working crewmembers to avoid customs. Since everything was in order, she went back to the hotel.

When she returned to the room, Mary still wasn't there. Since the balcony had a beautiful view, she decided to change into a robe, sit, and enjoy a glass of wine.

An hour later, the door opened, and Rosalyn knew Mary had returned, and hopefully had purchased the necessary items. It had been a long time since Rosalyn was able to relax and there was no longer a need to hurry things.

She sensed a presence behind her but never expected what happened next.

CHAPTER 51

Weeks later, Sergeant Charles Vickers contacted his counterpart, Special Agent in Charge, Billy Peters, at the Georgia Bureau of Investigations in Atlanta, and told him Judy Waverly's story.

Special Agent Peters was the lead investigator in the Georgia Bureau of Investigation and responsible for investigating criminal activity in the Atlanta area. Like Vickers, Peters was a veteran law enforcement officer with over twenty-five years on the job. He also possessed a suspicious nature when it came to criminal activity.

"That's ironic, Vickers because the body of Melanie Tifton was found in the trunk of her car two weeks ago. The car was found abandoned in the parking lot at the Silver Comet Trail just north of Atlanta. Joggers noticed the car when they arrived and still there when they left. The early morning enthusiasts never saw a runner on the trail and thought it strange the car was always there for several days."

"You're kidding me aren't you, Peters?

"Nope, they reported it to the Park Ranger, and when he investigated the incident, he found the vehicle unlocked. The Ranger was suspicious, so he thoroughly checked the car including the trunk. That's when he found Tifton's body. He contacted the State Police immediately."

"Was there a decisive match for Tipton, Peters?" Vickers asked.

"The ID was that of Melanie Tifton, but a search of her fingerprints revealed that she had many names and was a person of interest in many suspicious scams. One involved a bank officer named Linda Jacobs. Also, she had a brother and participated in scams with a Bill McPayne, whose whereabouts are unknown."

"Don't know any McPayne, but Linda Jacobs was found murdered in Blocker's Bluff not too long after her boss, Tom Parker, who owned the local bank, was found killed in his home. His wife, Barbara's whereabouts are unknown too," said Vickers.

"Damn, Vickers; that's an amazing coincidence especially with the Tifton/Parker connection. I'm going to check out Strategic Investments and will let you know what we find," Peters added.

Unfortunately, what Peters and his team found at Strategic Investments were unoccupied offices with no sign of their inhabitants. There were no computers and the only fingerprints they found belonged to Tifton,

Parker, Jacobs, and the investors. The file cabinets were empty, and there were no records of anything relating to any business operations.

When Peters contacted the investors, they told him of the land deal and how much they had invested—including the part about the bank deposit of $200,000. They also mentioned that there was another female, but the only description they could offer was a nice rack and very shapely legs! Unfortunately, they were suffering from a case of inattentive blindness.

A check with the building manager who rented the space said the only person he had contact with was the Tifton woman. As of yet, there was no sign of the brother.

Vickers searched his database and saw the report of a body of a male found in a Motel 6 off I-26, and it appeared to be that of Johnny Tifton. There was no sign of trauma, and the cause of death remains a suspicious nature.

He contacted Peters and gave him the news.

"Have you run the fingerprints yet, Vickers?"

"Yeah, hold on! Well, guess what? They belong to one of the Tifton woman's aliases. It looks like we found the brother, wonder who did him in?"

"Probably the same person who did Tifton. It seems everything connects to her. We know she's related to McPayne. So far he doesn't appear to be involved, but that doesn't mean he isn't," replied Peters.

"You're right. We don't have any idea of McPayne's whereabouts or the Parker woman. Is it possible that she's connected to him also?"

"Don't see how but one never knows. Have you got a BOLO out on her, Vickers?"

"Yes, and we just got a hit. Hold on."

Vickers checked his BOLO database and found a hit on Barbara Parker's vehicle from the Charleston Police.

"Her car was discovered in a 24-Hour Barbeque Spot's parking lot. The manager noticed the car parked there for several days and reported it to the Charleston Police. The investigating officer noticed the license plate was on our BOLO, so he wisely reported it. We sent a team out to investigate."

"Any report back yet?" asked Peters.

"We'll have it later today. I'll call you when I get it."

"Thanks, Vickers. You take care."

"You too, Peters."

Several hours later, the report came to Sergeant Vickers. The vehicle was dusted for fingerprints. Unfortunately, all the prints found belonged to Barbara Parker. The report noted that there was some blood on the passenger's side, and a DNA sample was taken.

The next day, Vickers got the result of the DNA sample. It was compared to samples taken from the Parker residence, and it was a match to Barbara Parker. Not only was she a missing person of interest, but now she was also the possible victim of a suspicious homicide.

Vickers called Peters and gave him the information.

The case or cases had taken on a whole new meaning. Both of them were now more curious about McPayne and the unknown woman.

Peters had already put out a BOLO on McPayne, but he couldn't do that with the woman. He told Vickers he would be laughed out of his job if he put out a BOLO on an unidentified woman described as having shapely legs and a nice rack.

They both had a good laugh, but were not amused by the dilemma.

CHAPTER 52

Three months later, Molly and Old George watched as Porter's boat approached the dock, waved to her and she waved back. Porter and Edison seemed content and were sporting shit-faced grins.

"Old George, it looks like they caught dinner. Good thing, 'cause I'm not in the mood to prepare a meal for four." Old George barked in agreement.

Porter tossed Molly the line, and she secured it.

"By the look on your faces, I'd guess you caught us a nice dinner for tonight. Good because I hadn't planned on cooking, especially for four." Molly called out.

Commander Edison laughed. "We caught some damn good ones. Don't worry Molly; I'll take care of cleaning and gutting them."

"Thanks, Commander, I know that old fool won't."

"Hey, I thought we were on first name basis? Please call me, Mo?"

"Okay! Thanks, Mo!"

While the men were fishing, Molly reminisced about her new fame after the drug bust, the Jacobs and Parker murders and their link to the one in Atlanta. She also received some credit for uncovering the bank embezzlement. Molly even had an interview with a TV reporter from a national cable television news network. The townsfolk called her a celebrity, although she didn't consider herself as one. Molly was also grateful for the credit the Commander and Sergeant Vickers gave her for her role in solving the cases.

Old George received an unofficial commission as a Master Chief Petty Officer in the Coast Guard. Commander Edison personally made the award. Old George accepted the commission with a proud salute.

There was no mention of Porter, but he didn't care, as he was both happy and proud of Molly. She deserved all the credit. What pleased him most was that Sheriff Stockton would be royally pissed that he didn't receive any mention at all.

Blocker's Bluff Bank didn't close entirely. The Office of The Commissioner of Banking in South Carolina seized control of it, and during their investigation, they uncovered the embezzlements. The one good thing that Tom Parker did was keep the FDIC insurance premiums up to date. The townsfolk's accounts were all safe.

Ed McClellan didn't get his mortgage but went to Charleston and was able to secure one from a local bank there. He completed the extension and hired five new employees. The online business was booming.

Barbara Parker was still missing and considered a possible suspect in her husband's murder. Her children were devastated over the events.

CHAPTER 53

The manager of the Palace Hotel's cleaning service reported to the hotel manager that her staff tried numerous times to clean room 436, but the 'do-not-disturb' sign was always on the door. She wanted to know if she should use her passkey.

The hotel manager said the guests had not checked out, nor have they requested any fresh linen, so go ahead and use the passkey.

When she opened the door, she knew right away something was wrong because the smell was horrible. She stepped in and immediately noticed the body on the bed, called the hotel manager, and told him to come right away. When the manager arrived, he saw the body and immediately called the Paradise Island Police.

Paradise Island's Police Department was adept at handling murder cases as they've done so in the past, but it wasn't as sophisticated like in the States. Fingerprinting was the first order of business then processing the body. The body then was taken to the Medical Examiner's office.

The hotel records indicated there were two guests registered for room 436, a Mr. and Mrs. Jansen, and neither had checked out. The Chief Constable asked if anyone had seen Mrs. Jansen.

The hotel manager checked with both desk clerks but only one remembered checking them in. The other remembered the woman going shopping one day, as did the man. When asked to describe Mrs. Jansen, all he could say was gorgeous legs and a big chest. Another case of inattentive blindness, just like in Atlanta.

The Chief Constable had to stifle a laugh as the description was of no help, and the only thing he had was a male's fingerprint. When he asked the cab drivers around the hotel, none of them remembered picking up a passenger fitting the female's description. The constable didn't expect to hear anything different.

The fingerprints turned out to be of no use as there was nothing in their database and the Constable didn't bother to check Interpol. As far as he was concerned, he had an unsolved death. The Medical Examiner missed the needle mark on Mr. Jansen's neck.

No one checked the bank Mrs. Jansen had used to wire funds. It wouldn't have done any good, since the female bank officer who handled the transfer certainly wouldn't have made notice of her customer's legs and chest. Her male counterparts, however, may have, but this woman was intelligent and responsible.

The incident was recorded as a mysterious unsolved death with an unidentified potential witness, and possibly a kidnapping. The Chief Constable didn't need that on his plate, so he filed the incident report and left it at that. When he finished, he left to go to his son's soccer match.

Mr. Jansen, a.k.a Bill McPayne was buried in a potter's field because Paradise Island wouldn't pay for a formal burial. No one would ever know what happened to Bill McPayne.

Ultimately, the authorities in the States traced the wire transfers. Unfortunately, the trail ended because the funds were all withdrawn as cash. Where the money went, they had no idea. Even the money used to pay for the charter boat was untraceable.

EPILOGUE

Much had changed in Blocker's Bluff since the events that took place five years ago. The Bank of Blocker's Bluff was now a branch of East Coast National Bank. The large regional bank acquired it from the State not long after the Office of the Commissioner of Banking seized it. It was in the bank's interest since they were the lender on the development loan for the Coastline Resort Community project.

Blocker's Bluff had grown since the advent of the Coastline Resort Community west of town. Parker's original investor had shied away from the original deal but when things quieted down, he approached the owners of the land, Daniel and Rosemary Parker, who acquired the property in their inheritance from Tom Parker.

His group purchased the thirty-five hundred acres and another five hundred owned by Molly Dickson and Willie Dawson. They each owned two hundred fifty acres inherited from their paternal grandparents.

As it turned out, Willie and Molly were related. Parker's Grandfather gave the land to their grandparents after the 1916 hurricane. Both had worked for the elder Parker and were responsible for saving his son from drowning as a result of the floods. The land was a token of his appreciation.

The Bank's new branch manager was Rosemary Parker, the daughter of Tom and Barbara Parker. After graduating from The University of South Carolina in Columbia, she took a job with East Coast National in Charlotte in their Branch Manager Training Division.

Rosemary received letters from Chief Molly Dickson, Sergeant Vickers, and acknowledgment from The Office of the Commissioner of Banking that she and her brother had made restitution for the embezzlement by their father. She was cleared of any implications and exonerated for her parents' sins.

Rosemary quickly rose to an Assistant Branch Manager position in Charleston, and when the position in Blocker's Bluff opened, she put her name in for transfer. Even with the stigma from her father, the Bank recognized that since she was originally from the town, they made her the top candidate and given the position.

Development of the resort had commenced three years ago, and the golf course was already functioning. Some homes had been completed and sold. Many of the townsfolk were employed there.

Thanks to the development of the resort community and the town's growth, electrical power and telephone lines were buried underground doing away with the unsightly poles. The resort's developer covered most of the costs. Blocker's Bluff residents were happy to see the poles and lines gone.

The resort developer constructed a new permanent dock and erected a seawall to help prevent flooding from future storms. The developer also built a marina for visitors who came by boat.

Several of the vacant buildings were now retail shops. There's a gift shop, a ladies apparel shop, and a travel agency to name a few. Downtown Blocker's Bluff was now a vibrant place to shop and visit.

Thanks to Molly's television interview and several newspaper articles, the town became a curiosity seekers paradise. Hundreds came to walk through town, have lunch, sometimes dinner at the restaurant, and to shop at the general store purchasing postcards and fresh baked goods.

Miss Mavis had postcards made with a picture of the downtown and *"Greetings from Blocker's Bluff"* imprinted on them. Even the gift shop sold them.

The developer also constructed a new four-lane paved road that connected the town and the resort community to I-95. Blocker's Bluff was gradually becoming a vibrant coastal community.

The town's population had more than doubled to 2,000 and with the advent of new citizens both seasonal and permanent, the crime rate tripled. Three tickets were issued for failure to come to an appropriate stop at the four-way stop sign in the center of town. As a result, the Town Council had a stop light installed, and so far the crime rate was back to normal.

The opening of a Super Wal-Mart in Beaufort was also a blessing for the town. Many of the townsfolk worked and shopped there alleviating the drive to Charleston.

No criminal charges were filed against Judy Waverly for what she knew and told the authorities. Sergeant Vickers had kept his word. Judy was now a member of the sales force at the resort and doing just fine.

Chef Willie purchased the restaurant and the general store from the Parker children and renamed it Willie's. The restaurant was more popular than ever as everyone appreciated Willie's cooking skills.

He added additional seating capacity of thirty and purchased some much-needed equipment for the restaurant and bakery. The new residents and visitors savored his culinary delights. The general store expanded by adding more goods that were popular with the local youth, like candies and ice cream. Also added, were some additional over the counter medications and, of course, postcards.

Miss Mavis hired a waitress for the restaurant who also helped in the general store. She was a local girl, who after high school didn't have the grades to get into college, so the waitress job was perfect for her. She also had a young child.

The girl's mother and the Mayor started a day care center for several of the young women who needed to find jobs to help support their families. Some worked in

Beaufort, and some found work in Crofton. Their husbands also found work away from town. It was a convenience for all.

Chef Willie hired a dishwasher to ease the burden on Miss Mavis. Melvin Washington was a veteran who was injured by an IED in Afghanistan and later discharged. Willie had been training him to be a cook and the young man frequently went fishing with Porter and Eddie McClellan.

The Town Council had also gone through significant changes. Gone were the white members who forced Porter out. Judy Waverly and Ed McClellan Senior were elected, as was Billy Marsden. The new Council looked more favorably on John Porter.

New Mayor, Wilma Patterson was a retired schoolteacher who had taught for thirty years at Crofton County High. She became a savvy politician and a shoe-in for the job. Her husband was a supervisor at the CCUC plant.

The town even had a practicing physician. The Mayor's daughter, Edna Myers, returned to her roots and set up an office in the veterinary's office. Now, it was like a two for one package, and it reduced her overhead. When the vet retires, which would happen soon, she'd take over the entire space. Her husband, Robert was the head project manager for the whole Coastline Resort Community. Moving back to Blocker's Bluff was convenient for both of them.

Dr. Myers was a practicing pediatrician and had privileges at the Crofton Regional Hospital and

Beaufort Memorial Hospital where she was on both of
their pediatric staffs. The income offset the little that
she earned in Blocker's Bluff as the vet and the local
doctor. She was more about serving the community than
getting rich.

The Myers moved into Parker's old house. Mr. Myers
imposed two conditions. No arguing in the house and no
vases. Both were a little reluctant at first but moving into
the house was an absolute necessity if they wanted their
characters included in this book.

The Police Department had also grown. With the
growth of the town, the Town Council authorized Molly
to hire two deputies. Molly hired one deputy and an assistant who managed the office when Molly was out. Adrian
Williams later became an Assistant Police Officer.

The Senior Deputy, Eddie McClellan, was being
groomed to become the next Chief of Police when Molly
decided to retire, which wasn't too far in the future.
McClellan joined the department after finishing a tour in
Afghanistan followed by two years of Junior College.

Reluctantly, and with the urging of Molly, Porter
eventually gave way to progress and sold off some beachfront property to the Coastal Resort Community develop-
ers. With the proceeds of the sale, he demolished the old
cabin and with the help of Eddie McClellan, his newfound
friend and also a contractor from Beaufort, he built a new
one with all the necessary modern amenities.

They built the new cabin on sturdy stilts in the event
of a severe storm. Porter also purchased a brand new bed.

Porter and McClellan bonded after Porter convinced Molly to hire him. Porter understood what he was going through after returning from active military duty.

Both saw action and shared a wartime bond, even though the two wars were decades apart. It was natural that they'd become good friends, regardless of their ages. It was something many veterans of past and present wars were doing nowadays. It was happening all over the country, unlike after the Vietnam War ended and the returning service personnel were spat upon.

McClellan's respect for Porter increased when Porter and Molly convinced Judy Waverly to sell McClellan the Jacobs' house. She had purchased it from the Jacobs' estate after the initiation of foreclosure proceedings.

None of the institutions involved wanted the house, especially with its history. Judy bought it at a bargain. She was happy to sell McClellan the house, especially since Porter and Molly still held on to Judy and Linda's secret.

Porter continued to propose marriage to Molly and finally one day she accepted. She figured she'd best do it before the old fool got too old to remember to ask her. Molly felt it was time to do what they should have done decades ago.

After everything that happened, Molly also felt that life was too short to dismiss what the heart always wanted. She was now known as Molly Dickson Porter. Chef Willie proudly gave her away at the wedding. She looked prettier than ever dressed in white and even blushed through the entire ceremony.

Sadly, Old George had gone to doggie heaven in the sky. He was Porter's best friend for a long time but his time had come. Porter got a new dog, a female Golden Lab. Molly got to select the gender, but Porter insisted on naming the dog, Miss Molly.

Now, just like Old George, Miss Molly goes for walks with Porter and is with him when he goes fishing. Both Mollies have new beds and Porter now has two women in his life.

Porter loved to tease them both and would often call out, "Molly!"

His wife would answer, "Yes, you old goat! What is it?"

Miss Molly would come and wave her tail.

Porter would laugh and say, "No, the other Molly!"

He did it so often that one night after dinner while Molly was in the kitchen putting dishes away, he tried it again, but both Mollies ignored him.

"Hey, can a guy get a beer here?" he yelled.

"Get it yourself, old man!" Molly shouted, and Miss Molly barked.

"Geez," Porter said and got it himself.

Now whenever he wanted a beer, he had to get up and get it himself.

One evening during one of their walks, Mrs. Porter accidentally made a little toot.

"What the hell was that, Molly?" asked Porter.

"My ass caught your cold and sneezed," she replied with a smile. All three of them laughed.

Barbara Parker never surfaced; neither did the mysterious woman with the gorgeous legs and big chest.

Bill McPayne was still a person of interest whose whereabouts were unknown.

Molly continued to read fiction novels and had just finished reading a new release about the Sheriff of a small town on the coast of Mississippi. The town was called Parkersville. She found it amusing that the sheriff's character was almost like John Porter, even with his dog. Even the plot was a little similar to what took place in Blocker's Bluff.

Commander Edison also found the novel amusing even the character that slightly resembled him.

Sergeant Vickers was a recent convert of fiction and was also enjoying the book. As he read it, he too often commented how eerily similar the storyline was to the events that took place, including the missing wife.

Eddie McClellan and Rosemary Parker posted their engagement announcement on their Facebook page. Shortly after that, Rosemary received an engagement gift from an anonymous source. The gift was a locket that was similar to one her mother gave her when Rosemary turned sixteen. For some strange reason, she would cherish the gift.

Somewhere, someplace, the author of the fiction novel, *Parkersville*, was sitting on the porch enjoying a cup of coffee, relishing the success of the book written using several pseudonyms to remain anonymous. Even the agent's name was a pseudonym. The book was first published using a self-publishing company, and then later picked up by one of the distinguished publishing houses.

With a cup of coffee in hand, the author watched her in their garden cutting flowers for the dining room table, as she often did. The garden had blossomed with her care. She seemed to have a magic touch when it came to gardening. Everything she planted bloomed profusely.

When she turned, she smiled and gave the author a little wave.

On the porch, the author smiled and waved back.

AUTHOR'S NOTE

This book is a work of fiction and people, names, characters, places and incidents are the product of my imagination or used fictitiously. Any resemblance to actual events, locales or persons, living or dead is entirely coincidental.

Blocker's Bluff was originally published in 2013. It was my first foray into writing and publishing a book. Since then I have written and published two more—one an award winning novel.

I decided to revisit Blocker's Bluff and make some changes before I published my next book. The characters are the same as is the plot, but the writing style was improved.

I'm often asked why South Carolina? Good question. I could have picked any coastal state, but my mindset was in South Carolina when I started writing this book, and Blocker's Bluff was where and how I pictured the town to be. Crofton and Blocker's Bluff exist only in my head and on paper.

I write fiction not fact. It's what I enjoy doing—making things up as I go along.

Thanks to numerous Internet search engines, I was able to research them for background information. Many cities, towns, counties, state and federal websites also provided background information.

I took the liberty to embellish most of the information I learned to add flavor to the plot. I may even have distorted events and facts a little. Maybe more than a little! Okay, way more than a little!

I also reached back into my ancient and extensive banking background for some help.

I'd be remiss if I didn't thank those who offered valuable suggestions. They were extremely helpful.

By now you recognize that this book was about greed and with greed comes unsavory characters, unsavory deeds, unpleasant language and that other thing that ends with an x.

Happily, dogs are still man and woman's best friend and companion, and old dogs still go to doggie heaven in the sky. As for me, I'm still an old man enjoying everything life offers, good or not so good.

As I have said, this is purely a work of fiction, and there are no resemblances to real characters.

I had fun making up the characters and creating the various plots.

That's what life's all about, having fun!

Thanks for reading my book. I hope you enjoyed it and will recommend it to your friends. Feel free to post a comment on Amazon or a reply on my website, www.georgeencizo.com and find my other books.

Made in the USA
Charleston, SC
10 March 2017